parABnormal Magazine

June 2024

Edited by H. David Blalock

parABnormal Magazine
June 2024

All rights reserved. No part of this book may be reproduced or transmitted in any form or by any means, electronic or mechanical, including photocopying or recording or by any information storage and retrieval systems, without expressed written consent of the authors and/or artists.

parABnormal Magazine is a work of fiction. Names, characters, places, and incidents are products of the authors' imaginations. Any resemblance to actual events or persons, living or dead, is entirely coincidental. Story and illustration copyrights owned by the respective authors and artists.

>   Cover illustration by Shawn Howe
>   Cover design by Laura Givens
>   First Printing, June 2024
>   Hiraeth Publishing
>   http://www.hiraethsffh.com/
>   "This Cat Must Die" originally appeared in Stupefying Stories 2014

Visit http://www.hiraethsffh.com/ for online science fiction, fantasy, horror, scifaiku, and more. Support the small, independent press...

Vol. VI, No. 2, Issue 22   June 2024

parABnormal Magazine is published quarterly on the 15th day of March, June, September, and December in the United States of America by Hiraeth Publishing, P.O. Box 1248, Tularosa, NM, 88352. ©2024 by Hiraeth Publishing. All rights revert to authors and artists upon publication except as noted in selected individual contracts. Nothing may be reproduced in whole or in part without written permission from the authors and artists. Any similarity between places and persons mentioned in the fiction or semi-fiction and real places or persons living or dead is coincidental. Writers and artists guidelines are available online at www.hiraethsffh.com. Guidelines are also available upon request from Hiraeth Publishing, P.O. Box 1248, Tularosa, NM, 88352, if request is accompanied by a self-addressed ***10 envelope with a first-class US stamp. Editor: H David Blalock.

Contents

Stories
7	*Consignment* by Ann O'Mara Heyward
24	*Grandmother* by Cory Swanson
34	*The Man on the Stairs* by Paul O'Neill
45	*This Cat Must Die* by Jason Lairamore
57	*Underworld* by Paul Lonardo
75	*Inheritance* by Dale Kesterson
91	*Dead Ringer* – Part I by Herika Raymer

Poems
44	*Lamia* by Christian Dickenson
56	*The Hungry House* by Randall Andrews
74	*Why the Angel Dudley Didn't Want to Return to Earth* by Denise Noe

Articles
116	*Moralist to Seducer: How Fiction Inverted Dracula* by Denise Noe
122	*Exploring Occult Detective Fiction with Michael Fitz-James O'Brien* by Sonali Roy

Illustration
23	Photo by Lakmon Sevim
90	*Nature's Spreadsheet* by Sonali Roy

A Little Help, Please

In the world of the small indie press we fight a never-ending battle for attention to our work, as writers and in publishing. Here's an example: big publishers [you know who they are] have gobs of $$$ that they can devote to advertising and marketing. Here at Hiraeth Publishing, our advertising budget consists of the deposits for whatever soda bottles and aluminum cans we can find alongside the highways. Anti-littering laws make our task even more difficult . . .

That's where YOU come in. YOU are our best promoter. YOU are the one who can tell others about us. Just send 'em to our website, tell them about our store. That's all. Just that.

Of course, we don't mind if you talk us up. We're pretty good, you know. We have some award-winning and award-nominated writers and artists, plus other voices well-deserving to be heard [not everyone wins awards, right?] but our publications are read-worthy nevertheless.

That number once again is:

www.hiraethsffh.com

Friend us on Facebook at Hiraeth Publishing

Follow us on Twitter at @HiraethPublish1

What???

No subscription to parABnormal Magazine??

We can fix that . . .

Just go here and order:

https://www.hiraethsffh.com/product-page/parabnormal-magazine-subscription

...also makes a great gift
any time of the year

Consignment
Ann O'Mara Heyward

Kira hadn't liked the mirror, personally. But she had developed a discerning eye for what would sell, attending endless estate, moving, redecorating, divorcing and quietly-gone-bust-or-got-indicted sales scattered around Vero Beach and the barrier islands. Accepting or politely refusing items offered to her for resale by the well-heeled of the Treasure Coast or their disinterested heirs. Learning through lean years at the beginning that her taste didn't always align with that of her clients.

She thought the mirror was too ornate. Venetian, an antique over-the-top exercise with floral motifs and elaborate glass scallops arranged around beveled glass panels. But it was in perfect condition, without a chip or crack, and the price at the estate sale was a ridiculously low five hundred dollars. She knew Sarah, the estate liquidator; their livelihoods both involved the resale of gently worn possessions of the wealthy to those that aspired. "What's the story on the mirror?" she asked, and Sarah shrugged. "The heirs don't like it," she said. "The daughter said price it to sell. We did."

She would put it in her shop at two thousand, five hundred. She was confident it would leave her hands within a week at that price.

Tom, her moving contractor, didn't like the mirror either and didn't mince words. "Goddam thing bit me," he said when he brought it to the store, carefully wrapped and padded, and showed her a cut across his palm. "Be careful handling that thing." Two weeks later he was dead. He'd gone fishing in the lagoon. His hands had been in the water. *Vibrio vulnificus* had gotten into the cut and killed him, eating his flesh as it spread, from his hand to his arm to the rest of him.

She hoped the mirror would sell soon. Poor Tom. Mindful of his parting caution, she'd hung it on the wall of her shop with her hands in heavy suede work gloves. It was heavy, but she was stronger than she looked; the hours at the gym lifting weights to maintain her figure had paid off. She added an extra thousand to the final check she owed Tom for the past month's moves, including the mirror, and sent it to his widow. It didn't make her feel any better. Every time she caught sight of her own reflection in the mirror, she disliked what she saw. She looked hardened, cynical, rapacious. At complete odds with her mental image of herself as just another honest immigrant trying to run a business in Paradise.

***

A few weeks later, the mirror was still with her, watching her as she went about her work arranging, displaying, tagging the objects of her trade. She was thinner, she noticed as she passed it, eyes half-averted. Thinner and older. Thinner she didn't mind so much. Older wasn't great for business. People liked to buy beautiful things from beautiful people.

On Tuesday, Angela stopped in. Kira had been cultivating Angela for months. Her blonde, trim, tanned and fashionably togged image regularly appeared in glossy local magazine ads designed to secure buyers and sellers for her real estate brokerage. Angela had expensive tastes, but she was no fool. Angela appreciated Kira's consignment shop for its primary value: creating the appearance of wealth without necessarily having to possess it.

The mirror drew Angela immediately. "Where did you find this beautiful thing?" she asked, just brushing the edges with tastefully lacquered fingertips. "A house on one of the barrier islands," Kira replied. Angela flipped the dangling price tag over and looked at the figure. "Would you take two thousand?" Kira hesitated for just a moment, then smiled her brightest smile. "For you, yes." Thank God, she thought, I'll finally get rid of it.

Angela stepped over to Kira's desk with her credit card. "I'll need it delivered," she told Kira. "What's the name of your moving guy, again?"

Kira's face fell. "I'm without a mover right now. Tom

passed away unexpectedly."

Angela frowned. "He was just a young guy, wasn't he?" Kira nodded. "I guess you could describe it as an accident, but he got very sick, very fast."

"That's too bad," Angela said. Kira wasn't entirely sure if she meant Tom's death, or the inconvenience of having to arrange a different mover. "Well, I'll find somebody to pick it up and have them call you, then."

For the first time, Kira was glad to see Angela go. She was even happier to see the mirror go when Angela's mover picked it up three days later.

The mirror came back within a month.

***

Kira was at her desk, deep into researching auction values on Chinese porcelain, when her cell phone rang. Distracted, she just swiped to answer automatically. At first, she heard only the rushing sound of an open cell phone line, wind blowing in the background. She nearly hung up, thinking it was a wrong number, when she heard someone whisper her name. Then the call dropped. The caller ID showed Angela's number.

Kira hit the phone icon below the number to call back. Her call rolled over to Angela's cool, businesslike realtor voice, asking Kira to leave a callback number and promising earnestly that your call was *very important* and she would return it just as soon as possible.

She scrolled through the customer contact list on her laptop. There it was. Angela's address. A beachside condo on A1A, about 20 minutes away. She flipped the sign on the door from Open to Closed, got her keys, bag and phone, locked up, and got into her car. All these years in the U.S, and she was still inclined to check things out for herself *before* she called the police.

She didn't have to call them, as it turned out. When she reached Angela's oceanfront high rise, pulsing blue and red lights were already washing over the pale pink stucco exterior. A neon green ambulance was nearby. Kira felt a knot forming in the pit of her stomach. She parked in a visitor space and began walking to the entrance when she noticed a cluster of people, some of them crying and gesturing at the police offers standing nearby.

A police officer stopped her. "Do you live here, miss?" he asked. "No, " she answered. "I came because I got a call from someone who lives here. A client of mine. The call was strange, and she didn't answer when I called her back."

"And who is your client?" he asked.

"Angela Giannetti." The officer turned toward the cluster of people around the other police officers. "Simms," he shouted, beckoning with his arm. "Over here." The knot in Kira's stomach grew a jagged coating of ice. A police officer detached herself from the crowd at the entrance and walked over.

Kira answered her questions dutifully, without betraying impatience. Name, address, what was her relationship to Angela, the phone call that brought her here. Finally, Kira couldn't stand not knowing any more. "Please, can you just tell me what happened? Is Angela all right?" She was already confident that the answer to that question was no.

The two officers exchanged looks. The male officer shrugged.

Officer Simms spoke. "I'm sorry to tell you that Ms. Giannetti is deceased. We appreciate your answering our questions here, but we would like you to come to the station and give us a statement about her call to you. We're on Twentieth Street."

Kira nodded calmly, betraying no emotion. "Of course." It was never wise to antagonize the authorities. A lesson she had absorbed with her baby food.

A day after she gave her statement at the police station, the story of Angela's death reached the local news. Various outlets carried it, with varying degrees of breathless sensationalism. Some with barely concealed schadenfreude. Angela had been young, wealthy and attractive. People, Kira thought, couldn't resist a story of something terrible happening to someone who had everything.

Angela had gone over her condo's seventh floor balcony railing and landed on the concrete pool deck below, in front of a dozen horrified witnesses either in the pool itself or lounging on poolside chaises. Some of whom spoke to the media off camera, on the condition that their names not be used. And no wonder. Kira was sickened at one account, comparing Angela's landing poolside to a smashed watermelon.

A week later, Kira attended Angela's memorial service. There was no casket; instead, a large portrait photo of a smiling Angela on an easel stood next to a table filled with expensive flowers surrounding a tasteful silver urn. Kira was surprised how few people were there. Angela had been prominent in the community, involved with multiple worthy non-profit boards. Aside from any other motivations, the visibility and connections had certainly been good for her real estate business. Her death was ruled a suicide by the coroner; apparently, at least one witness saw Angela climb onto her balcony railing, sway back and forth gracefully like a circus performer for just a moment, arms outstretched, then swan dive to the concrete below.

Which cleared Angela's husband Marco, who had been home at the time. Kira had met him briefly a few times at various social events. At the brief memorial service, he sat alone, dark glasses concealing his eyes, hands dangling loosely between his knees. Kira was reminded of a boxer sitting in his corner of the ring, too tired to get up and fight anymore. After the service, she sought him out to tell him how sorry she was.

She reintroduced herself when she reached him after the short line of mourners each shook his hand on the way out of the crematorium-cum-funeral home. Then walked away, shaking their heads.

She had just stepped away when she heard him speak to her again. "Hey," he said. "You're the one who sold Angela that mirror." His tone sounded accusatory. She turned around. "Yes, that's right."

"I want the goddam thing gone. Today." he said flatly. "I never want to see it again."

"Was there some problem with it?" she asked, keeping her tone calm and even. The man had certainly been through something terrible; it was enough to make anyone act strangely.

"I guess you could say so," Marco spat. "I think it killed her."

Kira stared at him, dumbfounded. She realized her mouth was open and shut it with a snap she felt in her molars.

"She stood in front of the damned thing, staring at herself, for at least an hour that day. I called her name; she didn't even hear me. She was in some kind of fucking trance. Then she turned away from it, finally. She looked straight through me, smiled, and walked out to the balcony. I saw her make a call; then she dropped her phone by her feet. I saw her climb onto the railing. All I could look at was her bare feet, flexing on that railing, rolling back and forth to keep her balanced. I was afraid if I tried to grab her, she'd fall. I shouted her name again and again, but...you know the rest. Along with everyone else in southeast Florida."

She knew there was no reasoning with him. Grief made people crazy. All she could do for Angela now was humor the man she left behind.

"I'll take it away," she said. "When would you like me to pick it up?"

"Now," he said. "I'm going to go have a drink. My lawyer is there at the condo. I'll call him to let you in."

Wordlessly, she turned away, got into her car and drove to Angela's seashell pink building. Her heels tapped in the cool marble entryway as she made her way to the concierge at a desk in front of the elevators. She gave her name and the unit number; he nodded, spoke briefly into his cell phone, then waved her on after she signed the guest log. No mention of what had happened. Kira reflected that one thing people in his job got paid for was their ability to keep their mouths shut. Not unlike her own business. When items came into her hands through misfortune, people didn't want others to know about it.

On seven, she stepped out of the elevator. A door opened on the ocean side of the hallway and a man stepped out to wait for her. "Kira?" he asked, putting his hand out to shake hers. "Bradley Summers. Marco's attorney. Thank you for coming. I'm sure you were surprised by the request."

"Yes," she said guardedly. "But grief does strange things to people."

"It does, indeed," he said, and ushered her into the apartment. It was breathtaking, of course; a glass sliding door opened onto the balcony, and beyond the balcony, the ocean rolled in all its blue and green magnificence. Automatically, Kira cast her eye around the room, identifying pieces by various designers. Whatever else could be said about Angela, she had cohesive taste; the room fit together in a harmonious whole that evoked the sea outside the windows.

Except for the mirror. Angela had had it hung on the wall opposite the windows giving on the sea; obviously, she'd meant to draw the reflection of the ocean inward into the room. But it was jarringly wrong for the room, Kira thought. Too ornate, too *much* for such cool, minimalist surroundings. Maybe Angela had liked the contrast.

Summers wasted no time. He gestured Kira to a seat on the white leather sofa, then excused himself to the hallway again with his cell phone. While she waited, Kira's thoughts swirled. None of this made any sense. Why had Angela called *her*, of all people, just before she jumped? Marco said she had been staring at the mirror. What was that about? And why would you gaze into a mirror, then kill yourself in front of your husband? She had liked Angela's hard-nosed practicality very much; they were kindred spirits in that regard.

Her train of thought was interrupted by Summers re-entering the room, flanked by two expressionless men in work uniforms. One carried an armful of quilted moving pads. Summers jerked his head at the mirror. The two workmen stepped forward. Two silent minutes later, the mirror was draped in pads, lifted from the wall, and carried out the front door to a waiting rolling cart.

Pointedly, Summers held the front door open, and looked at Kira. Message received, she thought; it was time to go. "I'll ride down with you," he said, and closed the door behind him. The hallway was already empty; the workmen must have taken a service elevator.

Alone in the elevator, Summers looked at Kira. "I'm sure I can rely on your discretion," he said. His eyes were the color of ice. "Mr. Giannetti is distraught, as I'm sure you can understand. It would be extremely unfortunate if any...speculation about his emotional state were to become known. And I'm sure the fact that he was distraught in relation to an item you sold Ms. Giannetti would not be helpful to you or your business. Nor would the fact that Ms. Giannetti called you shortly before her death. A refund of the mirror's purchase price will not be necessary. Consider it compensation for your trouble. Do we understand each other?"

"Absolutely," she said. Fucking bastard, she thought. What kind of idiot does he think I am, that he needs to threaten my business and bribe me to stay *quiet*? It's an insult to my intelligence. But then, she reflected bitterly, Americans sometimes heard a trace of foreign accent and automatically deducted fifty IQ points. Especially bastards like Summers.

The two workmen were waiting by the front door with their cart and the mirror. Summers walked out with all three of them, evidently ensuring that both the mirror *and* Kira were indisputably gone. Kira led the way to her SUV. The maintenance duo, silent as ever, lifted the mirror in its blanket of pads and slid it smoothly into the back of her vehicle. One man shut the hatch.

She got in, pushed the start button, and drove toward the exit to turn on to A1A. She glanced in her rear-view mirror. Summers was still standing there, watching her go. He's thorough, I'll give him that much, she thought.

"What am I going to do with you?" she asked the mirror. It rode in silence with her, back to the shop.

***

She re-hung the mirror on its hook in the shop carefully, again wearing heavy work gloves. She paused before hanging a new tag on it. I want it to *move*, she thought. And wrote the tag for one thousand dollars. *First Tom, then Angela. The mirror might be perfect – of its kind - but it had the feel of bad luck* about it. Superstitious idiot, she told herself. I guess you can take the girl out of Hungary, but you can't take Hungary out of the girl.

Her *nagymama* had an endless litany of superstitions and omens, down to what it meant if a black cat crossed your path going one way versus going the opposite direction. It was lucky if a spider landed on you. That one had given Kira pause when she was a little girl. She wasn't too crazy about spiders, honestly.

What had her grandmother said about mirrors? She thought back to the days of sitting at the kitchen table, eating cookies and listening to *nagymama* tell her stories. Nostalgia stabbed at her heart; she could almost smell baking sugar. *Nagymama* had died after Kira came to the States; at the time, she didn't have the money for the airfare to go back for the funeral.

Thinking about funerals reminded Kira what *nagymama* had said about mirrors. If someone died, you covered all the mirrors in the house or turned them to the wall. If you didn't, the soul of the departed could catch sight of their reflection, then become trapped in the mirror, looking out at the living ever after. Idiot, she chided herself. I loved her, but this is nonsense. Tales from an old lady told to a child.

But it gave her an idea. She wanted to know what happened to who had owned the mirror before it came to her. She would call Sarah about the estate sale; all she knew right now was that the previous owner was dead.

***

Kira met Sarah for coffee a few days later. There was a new place near the Village Shops in Vero she had been wanting to try; at least it would get her out of her own shop. And away from the mirror; its continued presence gave her a nagging anxiety, like a low-grade fever she could not shake. If the shop was busy, she could lose herself in chatting with customers. When it was quiet, she normally reviewed upcoming sale notices, photos of items customers wanted to sell, or researched pricing or provenance on the net. With that damned mirror on the wall behind her, she found herself constantly glancing over her shoulder. Especially if she was alone in the shop. Her thoughts were locked in an endless idiot circle.

Mirror, mirror, on the wall; did you cause a girl to fall?

The nights were worse, though. Before the mirror re-entered her life, she had usually dropped off within ten minutes of her head hitting the pillow. Now, her sleep was an uneasy doze penetrated by disturbing dreams.

Last night had been bad. She kept trying to turn her back to the mirror but the room spun around her, forcing her to turn and face it again and again. Finally, with the mirror before her, she struggled against the compulsion to open her eyes to meet her own reflection. In the illogic that only makes sense in dreams, she knew with absolute certainty it would be the death of her to catch a glimpse of her own face. She awakened trying to scream, dreaming that her eyes were being forced open.

She found a table. Her phone buzzed; Sarah texting she was running a few minutes late. While Kira waited, she scrolled through old emails to find the mirror's sale notice. Sarah handled so many, she wanted to be sure to ask about the right one.

Kira saw Sarah coming toward the coffee shop door. She exhaled. Unconsciously, she'd half-believed something would intervene and prevent their meeting. Enough, already, she told herself.

She rose to greet Sarah. They exchanged cheek kisses.

Sarah looked wonderful, Kira thought; she was wearing a dress Kira had seen in the window of a nearby boutique a few weeks before and hadn't even dared to price. Slim, tanned, healthy. In the mirror that morning, Kira's dark circles had been very pronounced. She had always had the delicate shadows under her eyes that many Eastern European women had; but today It had taken quite a bit of concealer to look even halfway decent.

Sarah's first words didn't help. "Kira, what's wrong? You look like you haven't been sleeping."

"Nothing, really," Kira answered, forcing cheer into her voice. "Just some things with the shop. Let's get our coffee and a little something, and I'll tell you. It's kind of funny."

The server made his way to their table, expertly twisting and turning between closely placed two-tops. They gave him their orders. Kira kept the conversation light – mutual acquaintances, the current show at the Vero Beach Museum of Art - until his return.

Coffee and plates in front of each of them, Sarah looked at Kira directly. "OK, give it up," she said, smiled, and waited.

Kira took a deep breath. "You know that estate sale about seven weeks ago? Where I bought that Venetian mirror?" Sarah nodded. "I know this is a really strange question, but what happened to the owner? I know it was an estate sale – you said the heirs didn't want the mirror – but if you don't mind my asking, how did he die?"

Sarah's smile faded immediately. "You know my clients expect confidentiality," she said. Kira nodded. "I promise you, our conversation stays at this table," she said. "I have my own reasons for wanting this to stay quiet. Maybe I should tell you first why I'm asking, but I didn't want you to think I was…well…imagining things." *Or thinking I was flat-out fucking crazy,* is what I really meant, isn't it? Kira thought.

She told Sarah, as briefly as possible, about Tom's cut and his death, Angela's call before she died. She left out what Marco had told her, other than that she had taken the mirror back at his request. "Ever since," she finished, "I can't seem to shake the feeling that that mirror is bad luck, somehow. So, I was wondering, what happened to the person who owned it before?" *Please tell me he died peacefully in his sleep at the age of one hundred*, she thought.

Sarah still hesitated, biting her lip as if trying to keep from speaking. "This conversation never happened, OK?" she said. Kira nodded again, her right hand going up unconsciously, as if swearing an oath. "The owner died in an accident. He was only fifty-six."

"What kind of accident?" Kira asked. Her mouth was going dry; she sipped her coffee. The ice-covered knot in her stomach was back; the coffee was not melting it. *We are getting to be old friends*, she thought.

"Well, the accident itself wasn't a secret," Sarah said, and winced. "Do you remember hearing about a bad accident at the airport?" Kira nodded. She *did* remember what Sarah was talking about, at least superficially. A man had been killed near the private aviation terminal. She didn't immediately recall his name; the reports had identified him as a successful Vero Beach entrepreneur with global business interests. She searched her memory, unsure of the details. "He was struck by some piece of equipment, wasn't he?" Kira asked. Sarah shook her head. "Close," she said, "but it was the other way around. Mr. McDonald walked straight into a spinning propeller."

"My God," Kira gasped. "His poor family."

"Yes." Sarah said. "And not just them. An aircraft mechanic was standing right there, as it happened. He told the investigators that Mr. McDonald came down the steps of the jet he came in on, then stripped to the waist. He laid his jacket and his shirt on the tarmac. Then he started walking toward a plane that was starting up, preparing to taxi. A few feet away, he put out his arms like a little boy playing at being an airplane and ran straight at the propeller, grinning from ear to ear. The mechanic was sprayed with blood and...tissue. So were others nearby, but he was the closest and saw it happen. He hasn't worked since. He's being treated for PTSD. He got a lawyer and sued the estate, for irreparable psychological damage caused by Mr. McDonald's actions. The daughters decided to liquidate everything here and give the mechanic a financial settlement. All parties agreeing not to disclose the terms."

"How long did Mr. McDonald have the mirror?" Kira asked.

"Not long at all. It was on board the aircraft. He bought it on his last trip."

***

Kira drove to the beach at Treasure Shores. She needed to clear her head. There was no way she wanted to go back to the shop right now. Not after hearing what happened to McDonald. She could just see him, bare-chested, arms extended atilt, making an airplane noise like a little boy as he ran, apparently joyously, toward his death.

She changed her heels for flip-flops, locked her car, then followed the boardwalk to the sand and the rolling blue ocean. A mile of footprints later, in the hard packed sand just above the waterline, she was no closer to knowing what to do, arguing with herself.

You cannot sell it to anyone else.

This is insane. I need to make a living. I've been around the damn thing off and on for weeks now and come to no harm. Other than a few bad dreams. There is no such thing as a curse.

Tell that one to nagymama. And see her shake her head in sorrow at you, for ignoring ancient wisdom you snicker at as superstition.

And even if it is cursed, what the hell does it want? Most "curses" I ever heard of were in revenge for something bad to start with. Betrayal. Murder. Carelessness. Injury, to body or soul or psyche. Whatever. A "curse" amounts to getting even. Rebalancing the scales. An eye for an eye. And is that completely wrong?

It is if it hurts innocent people who didn't do anything

bad. If it hurts only the guilty, maybe not so much.

Yes, but Tom and Angela. Neither was a bad person. What could they possibly have been guilty of? Or McDonald, for that matter?

Maybe it doesn't care.

Jesus, listen to yourself. A mirror having thoughts or feelings...my God, you are going off the deep end with this crazy shit. Stop it.

Yes, but three people are dead. And those are only the ones that you know of.

I didn't kill them.

But if you know something will cause harm, and you put it in someone's hands, you're complicit. They died in terrible ways. Tom suffered before he died, his flesh painful, then dead and rotting on his body. Angela died smashed and broken, all beauty and dignity fled. McDonald was...vaporized, sprayed all over everything and everybody nearby.

Suddenly, Kira smelled the seaweed rotting above the high tide line. She doubled over; the coffee and pastry of an hour ago came up with a liquid rush of bile onto the sand. She straightened, scrubbed her mouth with the back of her hand and turned back. She began retracing her steps along the shoreline. Unbidden, her thoughts resumed chasing each other.

The mirror is old. And fragile. But it survives.

Yes, but it needs human agents. To hang it on a wall. To buy and sell it. To get it from one owner to the next.

That's the only reason you've been safe, Kira. It needs you. To help it do its work.

And what if I refuse?

You know the answer to that question.

***

That night Kira dreamed of *nagymama*. She lay with her head in her grandmother's lap, in a field of wildflowers and grasses, smelling sweet in the sunlight. Her grandmother was stroking her hair. The weight of her hand on Kira's forehead was comforting. Kira's eyes were closed. The sun was warm upon her face. The only sounds were the breezes rustling the grass around them, crickets, and birdsong. She had never been so happy. So safe.

Her grandmother's voice, soothing, murmuring. *It's not so bad, being dead, you know. Especially if you choose for yourself how it will be. Most of the fear of dying comes from not knowing what will happen to you.*

Yes, she told her grandmother, being able to choose is important.

Choosing how is important. But it's even more important to choose why, her grandmother whispered. *The best deaths are for the lives of others.*

I remember. You told me that you learned that during the fighting. But you didn't choose then.

No. But at times I wished I did. Even though your mama was little then and needed me. I wondered if it was right. Not choosing.

It's hard to know what's right, Kira said.

Yes, it is.

They were silent together in the grass again. A bee buzzed as it circled a flower. It sipped the nectar as the breeze bent the stem first one way, then the other.

***

Kira woke knowing what she had to do. She rose and began her preparations, lips compressed in a thin line. Shower. Clean her teeth. Dress. Drive to the shop. Open the hatch of her vehicle, leave it waiting like an open mouth. Unlock the shop door. Prop it open. Put the heavy work gloves on. Lift the mirror carefully from the wall. Carry it to the car. Lay it in the back. Close the hatch, then get in and drive to where she was going.

She turned onto the Wabasso Causeway Bridge from U.S. 1 a little after sunrise. There were few cars, but a few early fishermen cast their lines from the pedestrian walkway into the water below. She pulled over at the highest part of the bridge, put the car in park, reflexively glanced in her review mirror, and carefully got out. She almost laughed; it would be the supreme irony if she were mowed down by a passing car before she could get rid of the mirror.

She raised the hatch again. She didn't bother with the gloves this time. Very shortly, the mirror's ability to hurt anyone else would be ended, in pieces on the bottom of the Indian River lagoon. She would accept the seven years' ill luck its ruin would bring; it would do far more damage intact. She balanced it carefully against her chest, arms clasped around it, and walked to the edge of the bridge. She let it slide through her arms and fall sixty feet, its weight plummeting straight into the water. Its bottom edge cleaved the water and it disappeared into the silt and sea grass.

Kira looked straight ahead. Instead of the wide, sparkling expanse of the Indian River, the sunlit meadow of her dream was before her. Above the waving grasses, the insects of the field caught the light, tiny motes dancing in the air. Behind a stile, her *nagymama* stood waiting, one hand shading her eyes, the other hand smoothing her apron. She smiled at Kira and opened her arms. Kira climbed over the stile and walked toward her. It was good to see her again.

***

Special to *Florida News*

*Vero Beach Businesswoman Jumps
from Wabasso Bridge in Apparent Suicide*

VERO BEACH – The body of area businesswoman Kira Almasy was recovered this morning from the Indian River Lagoon, just below the Wabasso Causeway Bridge. Witnesses reported that just after sunrise yesterday, a driver pulled over and stopped in the eastbound right lane of the bridge at its highest point. A woman later identified as Almasy exited the stopped vehicle and removed a large object from its cargo compartment, dropping it over the side of the bridge into the Indian River below. She then climbed over the three-foot tall concrete barrier at the edge of the bridge and stepped off. Police and emergency personnel responded to multiple 911 calls regarding the incident. Almasy was pronounced dead at the scene after police divers recovered her body from the water this morning.

Local fisherman Mel Lewis was fishing from the bridge when the incident occurred. "I don't know what she dropped in the water," Mr. Lewis stated, "but I saw it slide out of her arms, and it cut her to ribbons. She was covered in blood. I started toward her to try to help her, but I was too far away to reach her before she went off the bridge."

Police divers also recovered a large, ornate mirror from the water at the location of the incident. Remarkably, police said it was undamaged.

The comparatively low barrier at the edge of the bridge has been a source of concern to area pedestrians and cyclists for several years, who cite the relative ease with which a person could be knocked off the bridge into the water by an automobile. This tragedy will add to that controversy.

In an unrelated incident at the same location, several fishermen reported a substantial fish die-off near Wabasso Causeway Park which occurred the same day. Snook, redfish, and flounder were among dead fish of all sizes, which numbered well over a thousand.

Photo by Lakmon Sevim

Grandmother
Cory Swanson

Grandmother wasn't always so old. Years ago, she survived cancer. Decades before that, she quit smoking, went fishing, lost her husband. Life stuff.

I'm old now, too. How old, I can't remember. Time seems to dilate and contract here in this place where we take care of her. There's no telling how much has passed. There seem to be days and nights, but I'm certain sometimes a year has passed before the sun goes down, the curtains finally darkening and granting us our rest.

The temperature never changes, thanks to the machines humming on the roof, and outside always looks the same. There's a concrete sidewalk and the side of another brick building. Sometimes there's rain or snow, but it's hard to track the seasons. I mostly shut the curtains.

I remember when there was flesh on her. We worried when her knees started hurting too much to use her walker. Seems funny now. She hasn't walked in years. Decades? Who knows.

My point is, the flesh wasted away. It took time. I couldn't see it from day to day, never would have been able to pinpoint just when it happened.

All I know is, I've spent an eternity watching to see if this next breath will be her last.

She reaches for my hand and I oblige, the smooth, white bone cold in my hand. She doesn't know who I am, but she knows what I am. I'm the caregiver. I'm the one who looks out for her.

She doesn't want me to leave.

***

Janet visits on occasion. My sister lives several hours away. She works full-time and has two kids and an estranged husband, so it's often a stretch between visits.

She'll come sit with grandmother, her kids playing cards on the floor. She brings treats: chocolate from the store, tomatoes from her garden. I accept them politely, telling her I'll give them to grandmother when she's having a good day.

"You look terrible," she says to me in the hallway.

I nod, knowing the reality but not acknowledging the implication.

"You can leave. Go take a walk. Get some fresh air."

"She doesn't want me to leave," I say.

Her mouth hardens. "You have to take care of yourself."

"She needs me."

Janet's head falls. "You're a saint, Jeff. You're doing what nobody else in the family can do, but you're wasting away."

I have indeed grown gaunt. The food here isn't great. I've become lean from a lack of desire to eat.

"It's okay if you have some of the chocolates, too," she says, kissing me on the cheek before gathering her kids up and leading them back to her car.

The chocolates will probably end up in the trash.

***

Grandmother's yellowed teeth clack together, begging for water. I've long since put away the cup with the straw. She fought so mightily for so long just to suck the moisture past her dry lips.

Now I simply spoon it between her teeth. Who knows what happens to it after that point? Perhaps it splashes against her spine, moistening the white bone. Perhaps it dribbles into the sheets. Either way, it makes her happy.

I've often heard it said that we leave this life as we came into it. We're helpless and disoriented, dependent on others for every bit of sustenance and warmth.

Tears come often when I think of the woman she used to be. Grandmother taught us how to be proud, how to be ourselves. She was a cult of personality and I fell into her trap with all my heart. Some days, even after she'd lost her hearing, she'd go on and on about her family. People I'd never known, who'd died long ago, but who I knew in vivid detail through her stories.

She'd tell me how she'd loved her sister, Ruth. "She lived to almost one-hundred-and-one," she'd say. "I'll get her, though."

I can't do the math anymore. It feels as though she passed that mark years ago.

Then there was Betty. "She betrayed the family, running off to Texas with that man," she told me. "She was a mean person."

Nobody could hold a grudge quite like grandmother.

As with all her other organs, however, her brain softened as well. Dementia is its own form of forgiveness. It's hard to hold grudges when you can't remember your own family.

She's long since forgotten my name. It started with her confusing me for my dad or my uncle. Soon enough, though, she couldn't even do that.

"Who are you, then?" she'd ask.

I'd attempt to explain.

"You'll have to write it down for me someday," she'd say, trailing off.

I never did. It became useless to explain and her hearing was so dim, I simply told her that I'm her grandson.

Then came a long period of silence.

Then she stopped getting out of bed.

At this point, I could only see her hands and face, the rest of her body tucked under a thick layer of blankets.

It's been this way for quite a while. I can't even tell how long. If she asks my name again, I don't know what I'll tell her. I haven't thought about anything so trivial as my name in ages.

***

At one point, my uncle gave me my grandfather's rock hammer when he visited after cleaning out Grandmother's house. Grandfather had worked underground and fancied himself a small-time prospector, bumming around on BLM land looking for potential claims.

Grandfather died a long time ago. Grandmother never remarried.

I don't know why it surprised me that the hammer looked used. The point was worn and the blunt end was pocked from impact. A living person had used this tool. It bore the marks of his ambition, a poetry I've been trying to decode.

Here she is, Grandmother, still around. At least death had mercy on Grandfather. Death's inky cloak took him away long before we were ready. Why won't death come for her now? Why is she doomed to suffer long past her body's ability to sustain her?

I'm awakened from my reveries by the clacking of her teeth. Her hands rattle, reaching for the water.

I shift my weight in the little wooden chair beside her bed, my clothes long since too large for my emaciated frame.

Her demands are a torment, a constant waking into a bad dream. Her jaws reach up to the spoon, begging for the water. It spills between her yellowed teeth, which clack for more.

Once she's calm, I set down the spoon and glass. My own hands aren't what they once were. I used to be strong, fleshy even. There was a time I could do a hundred push ups. Now, the effort of giving her water has me breathing heavy.

I used to think I was here to comfort her as she slipped toward the end of her life. Now I know I never felt that way. I'm here to guard her, to scare away death. As much as I pray for her last breath, for the end of her suffering, the thought terrifies me. I'm not ready to let go.

Back when she was talking, she'd ask what time it was. The concept of time became more and more difficult to communicate to her. I often resorted to pulling the big, plastic clock off the wall and placing it right in front of her eyes.

"Oh, three-thirty," she'd say. "Why are you still here this late?"

"Because you need me," I'd reply.

"I'm fine," she'd tell me.

I couldn't find it in my heart to disagree, but she wasn't. She isn't.

For the longest time, I've wondered what's connecting her bones anymore. The flesh is long gone, the sinew and tissue a mere memory. I assume by the rise and fall of the blankets that she's still breathing, but I'm afraid to look under them. I don't want to see the emptiness of her ribs, her clothes rumpled over the nothingness beneath. I don't want to know what I've feared for so long.

Still, death does not come for her. So long as I'm by her side, he won't. He can't. How would he get past me? He'd have to take me, too.

I'm not ready for that. How do you say goodbye to someone who's been so important to you? How do you let go and admit their fire has been extinguished? I'm not ready for grief. I'm not ready for the stages: the bargaining, the acceptance.

It comforts her when I hold her hand. Her bones stop rustling and she relaxes. The carpals and metacarpals are cold in my palm. Her breathing slows.

It appears as though she's sleeping. It'll wake her if I take my hand away. I'm exhausted. It's late. I should go home or at least go sit in her chair and sleep.

But I'm not that selfish. I can't leave. It would kill her.

***

Morning comes and I haven't slept. Her hand is still in mine, the relative warmth of my flesh slipping into her bones. My butt hurts from the wooden chair and my body aches from holding its position, yet I dare not move.

"Mr. Ebbing," a nurse says in a half whisper from the door. "Are you all right?"

I look over, Grandmother's hand still in mine, feeling my own disheveled appearance and tangled hair. "I'm fine," I lie.

"Should we try some food? I've brought some broth."

The thought repulses me. "I'm fine, thank you."

"Not for you. For her."

Embarrassment washes through me and I let go of

Grandmother's hand. "Of course. How silly of me." I scoot the chair aside and let the nurse come to the bedside.

She didn't bring much, just a couple dribbles in a Styrofoam cup. The nurse attempts to get the spoon between her teeth, but Grandmother turns her head away.

"Come on," the nurse says. "It'll feel good."

Grandmother avoids the spoon again.

With dejection, the nurse sets the cup and spoon on the bedside table. "See if you can get her to eat. Otherwise, she doesn't have long."

The thought strikes me as the nurse leaves. I keep thinking Grandmother doesn't have long, that's why I've been here for what feels to be eternity. This little dance with the broth is one we've repeated day in and day out for months. Years? Yet she keeps going.

She's alive because I don't want her to die. How she's subsisting, I have no clue. I'm not forcing her to eat. The only thing she wants is water.

The bones of her hands rattle and the tips of her fingers scrape against her skull as she attempts to adjust the cannula feeding oxygen to her empty nasal cavity.

Frustration and anger pass through me. Why is she still here? How is this even possible? What is she living for? I've been waiting in steady vigil as everything about her rots away, but she's still alive.

My composure is lost. Tears stream down my face as I bury my head in the blankets on the edge of her bed. Anger and frustration and guilt surge through me in alternating waves. I haven't eaten, I haven't slept, I haven't bathed, all so I can be here with her through the end.

Grief is not allowed here, yet I'm awash in this miasma of emotion. Everything in me feels empty, time a vast chasm which swallows me. The sobs calm but the feelings do not.

Who knows how much time passes. The hand on my back serves as a punctuation, waking me from this vast canyon of self-pity.

I look up.

Standing next to me is a man. His clothes are neat and dark. "My, my," he says.

"Are you...?"

"Indeed," he says.

"Am I dead then? You touched me."

The man looks down. His head is bald but for a neat mustache. "Not yet. Funny how that rumor got started—the touching thing. It makes me seem like something you should be terrified of."

The feel of death is comforting. His hands are full and round and warm.

"I'm not afraid of you," I say.

"Nor should you be. I'm just another thing that happens. What we're really afraid of is saying goodbye. Most of our goodbyes aren't permanent, but this last one, well, it's a doozy."

I consider my position. I'm still between him and Grandmother. Death can't get to her while I'm around. Her hand is still clutching mine. "I'm not moving."

Death sighs, the outward spirals of his mustache twittering in the breeze of his breath. "You know, Jeffrey, dying is part of the natural order."

"I don't care." The empty sockets of grandmother's eyes stare at the ceiling, insensate of what's happening.

"So, you're going to block me—buy her time. I've been by on several occasions and you've been the same way. Do you think she's going to get better?"

I'm silent. He can't fool me with logic or words.

"It's supposed to be this way, Jeffrey. Far be it from me to lecture you, but what is it worth for her to hold on? Is she going to read a book? Go for a hike? Eat Christmas dinner with you?"

"None of that matters so long as she's here."

"It does matter, Jeffrey. Life is for living. Death is for dying."

Our words dissipate into the air and I'm left with only the hum of the oxygen pump.

"What's in front of you isn't her anymore," Death says.

"She's already gone. She's been gone. She just needs you to let go."

Grandmother squeezes my hand as though she's heard Death's words.

"Bones are not life. Flesh is life. Flesh fades."

The dim light of the digital clock beside the bed illuminates my hand. My own flesh has wasted away. It's grown gaunt and pale, my veins showing through the skin. Where has it gone?

"We are not made for eternity. We are crazy machines who rise and fall from the dirt. We take notice of ourselves and fade away."

The oxygen pumps and releases.

Grandmother squeezes my hand again. I know what she means this time. She wants me to be strong. "You take her over my dead body," I say to Death.

"Very well, then," he says.

I stand and turn around, pushing the chair out of the way. My clothes hang loose over my gaunt frame, but I attempt to look big, puffing my chest, hoping to scare Death away.

"Look at you, Jeffrey," Death says. "She's drained you as a spider drains a fly."

"You have to get past me," I say, my pulse beating in my ears. Death has no agency in this room, not without my permission.

In a moment, I am crumpled on the floor. Death steps over me and I grapple with his legs, too weak to impede him in any way. "Help," I manage to say, but my voice is too small.

Death leaves the room with a bundle of blankets in his arms, his crisp suit now the blue scrubs of the orderlies.

***

My sister's hand awakens me. Her eyes say everything that needs to be said.

I'm the one in the bed now. I'm the one with an oxygen cannula in my nose. It's my throat that's dry.

I squeeze her hand and she squeezes back, tears collecting in the corners of her eyes.

"Where is she?" I manage to say.

"She's gone."

My heart sinks. I did everything I could, but still she's gone.

"They said you haven't been eating."

I nod.

"Why not? You have to care for yourself before you care for others."

She deserves an explanation, but I'm too weak. I gave everything to Grandmother. Can't she see that?

Janet dries her tears. "I'm not here to scold you. They're going to help you get better."

"They?" I manage.

"Yes. The doctors and nurses."

"What about you?"

My sister lets go of my hand. "Jeffrey, I'll stay while I can, but you can't expect me to stay forever."

That's the thing, I do. Something in me boils. "Doctors and nurses aren't enough. I'll be alone. I'll be—"

"Calm down, Jeffrey."

"Please," I plea, hands shaking from the effort.

"Jeffrey, stop. I have a family. I have a job. You're not going to do to me what Grandmother did to you."

"What did she do to me?"

Janet stares down at me. "Look at you."

I do, seeing my frailty. Where I once had strong hands, I'm now little more than a skeleton. "She didn't do this."

"Really? You're wasted away. It was a trap. Now she's gone."

"She was our grandmother, not a..."

"Parasite?"

"But..."

"Not her whole life, but at the end. She became something else."

I sputter, looking for words and not finding them.

"You're not going to do it to me, Jeffrey."

It's not fair, what she's saying. In the end, I was too

weak to protect Grandmother any longer. She wasn't a parasite, I was her guardian. I was there to advocate for her. It worked, too. She lived for so long. She wouldn't have without me.

Janet gathers her purse. "Goodbye, Jeffrey. I'll come visit when I can."

I'm too weak to protest any longer. Everything inside me has withered and shriveled. Insult and anger boil in my guts. How dare she? What right does she have to walk out?

My sister plants a gentle kiss on my forehead. "Life is for living," she whispers, the familiar refrain now a bitter pill in my ears. "Death is for dying."

"Death leaves a heartache no one can heal, love leaves a memory no one can steal."
       ---From a headstone in Ireland

The Man on the Stairs
Paul O'Neill

The man stood at the top of the stairs again. The tall, shadowy stranger appeared every night, still as a dark statue. In the morning, he'd be gone, and the loneliness would seep back into Patricia's bones.

She stared up at the figure from the bottom of the stairs. "Will you ever open that mouth and finally speak to me?"

He didn't move. Just stood there, not breathing or anything. What pain caused him to haunt the cottage every night?

Maybe it was his long lost love he was waiting for. Maybe a lover broke his heart. Maybe he would wait forever.

"Maybe..." She itched at her forearm until it stung. "Wish someone felt that way about me. I'd love to hear what you sound like. Do you see me? I see you."

In the world outside the cottage and its low, wood beam ceilings, the April sun had set long ago, leaving its heat on the night air. Bugs chirped in the big garden.

The place was the opposite of Edinburgh in so many ways. Each house in the town of Drumnagoil seemed to have a field placed between it. She couldn't see her nearest neighbour. No street light hit her windows. The pale light that glowed into the house at night was from moon and stars.

"We could lay on the grass and watch the sky," she said to her mystery man. "Wish on a shooting star. What would you wish for? What's locked up in that heart of yours?"

Patricia set her hand on the oak banister. What did he look like under all that shadow? She could just make out the impression of his shape, but his features were phased out.

Some nights, she stood at his side, joining him as he focused on the floor downstairs. She couldn't tell exactly, but it looked as if he watched the front door, begging for someone special to open it. As she waited beside him, his presence tingled her skin, made the pit of her stomach feel funny.

When she'd bought the place a month ago, he'd appeared on her first night. She'd slid down the wall, clutching at her galloping heart. That reaction seemed silly now.

"Whoever it is you're waiting on," she said as she made her way up the stairs beside him, "they didn't know what they had. She left you in the cold. I could never do that. I'd take you outside and we could spin on the grass under a moonlit sky."

She had to flee Edinburgh to this town of Drumnagoil on the edge of Fife. They sold houses for tuppence here. The mumbling real estate agent with his crusty hair had showed her the cottage, told her how it was crammed with character. When she asked why it was so cheap, he itched his way through it, letting her know a few bad eggs lived here in the past. The house was still spoken about.

"Everyone's got their story," she'd said, already in love with the oak taint smell of the place, its low beams, the way the sun poured in through large windows.

He continued like he was trying to talk her out of it. Violence. Families ruined. Skeletons dug up in the garden. All this knocked ten or more grand off the asking price. Turned out she was the only one asking.

"You coming to bed?" she said, gazing up at her shadowy guest. "What colour are your eyes, I wonder? Bet they sparkle."

What would she do if he moved? If he reached out and took her wrist, drew her close, gave her a look full of wicked intent?

"Night, night," she whispered. "Whoever you are."

Despite the draught that fingered its way up to the bedroom from the front door and up those stairs, she kept the door open so she could see into the hall. From her pillow, she watched the man and his dark, lonely vigil.

Her eyes ached from trying to stay awake. The thought of him not being there in the morning was too much for her heart to bear.

***

The next day, after hours of tedious spreadsheet admin crap for her new boss as she hunched over her silver laptop, she set to furiously cleaning the kitchen.

The virtual world of Teams and working from home bothered her. Edinburgh would be abuzz by this time of night as everyone gossed in the pubs after work. It was probably a good idea she stayed in the virtual world for now. After what happened.

The tangy, orange-laced washing up liquid seemed to stay on her skin. Outside the kitchen window, the trees danced, all flowing in the same direction. She stretched, her bones cracking too hard for her twenty-seven years.

"Right, I'm off to bed," she called, loud enough for her guest to hear. "It sure would be nice to talk to someone on my way up. Someone who knows the place."

She nearly added *someone who could knock me off my feet*. The thought of it made a giggle creep its way out of her dry mouth.

The old floorboards creaked and cracked like thin ice as she stepped into the hall. "I'm all ears if you need some —"

He wasn't there.

The wind moaned at the front door behind her as she stood at the foot of the empty stairs. She waited. Maybe if she squinted her eyes in the right way, he'd come back to her. Her midnight stranger. Her watcher.

"Don't go," she said. "I haven't heard what you sound like yet."

Trying to sleep was impossible. Her blood felt like it wanted to float its way out of her, rise up to the ceiling, coat it in shifting, molten crimson. She got up, checked the stairs again, stood in his spot. Nothing. With him gone, she felt unsafe. Alone. By the time four o'clock in the morning came, she'd paced every corner in every room.

It made her make the midnight mistakes again. That's what she called it when she needed someone, anyone, in the wee hours. When she reached out on her devices to old friends, lovers, people she shouldn't.

She'd sent Robson a rushed, pulsing message on Facebook and then on email. They'd shared something special, no matter how it ended. No matter what his wife had screamed. Robson loved her deeply. He was just scared to fall into the fire of Patricia's embrace. So, he put on a show for everyone at work, earning her the sack.

The last time she saw Robson at the front door of his house in the middle of the night, he'd put on a show for his precious Delia. How could he possibly tell her how much he wanted to leave his wife in that situation? How he'd love to dig his nails into her back? Leave his bite marks?

"You're not right in the head," he'd roared as the summer rain soaked her through. "You're a headcase. A psycho. You've ruined everything."

She set her elbows on the cold kitchen table, put her head in her hands, pressing her fingers into her temples. It was like the floor had shifted under her, making her gut tumble.

She'd fallen for Robson at the Christmas night out. As they walked the slick, cobbled Edinburgh streets, he pulled her close. They'd made such beautiful, clutchy love in the alcove of a closed shop. In that moment, she'd been so sure she'd found the one. Her happy ever after.

It didn't matter how hard she plotted to drag Robson away from his wife. She had her hooks in him. The spindly old cow. How she longed to see the look on the wife's face when she stumbled on the gift Patricia had sent in the mail. Did she touch the lock of hair? The love letters? The used knickers?

That's when it all came out into the ugly open. That's when she decided to make a clean break of it, sell her pokey flat and buy this cottage in a place where the stars shone bright.

She stood at the top of the stairs in the spot where the man normally appeared. A pleasant chill flowed through her.

"Did I do something wrong?" she said. "Don't leave me

here all alone."

Outside, a tall tree moved, scraped the upstairs window with its long, dry fingers.

***

She stole naps during the most boring conference calls. A second night without her mysterious shadow man had her brain frazzled and useless. Did he see her and decide to vanish? Being abandoned by a ghost was a new low.

She tried finding out exactly what happened in this house, but the details were sketchy. A story about a family gone missing didn't touch the big papers in Scotland.

After work, she started on the vodka. It took everything in her to stop messaging Robson again. How would he react to finding out how obsessed she was with someone else? Someone tall, dark, handsome. Everything he never was. A man with staying power. A man who knew how to treat his girl. Knew how to wait at the top of the stairs and—

An ache in her wrist brought her back to the present. The Sharpie's alcohol smell stung her nostrils as she rubbed the centre of her palm. The words she'd written on the cream-coloured wall were swirly and smooth.

Lover boy, lover boy, where did you go? My lips are waiting for you. There's a sunset just for you and me.

Her lip quivered as she scored through the words, stabbing black marks through them. The tip made ear-splitting squeals as she pressed too hard.

"Stupid, stupid girl."

She needed some air. Needed out of this empty place.

The local boozer had three other customers. It smelled strongly of wet sawdust like an uncleaned hamster's cage.

There was a nice buzz creeping around her skull, blurring her ragged thoughts. She was halfway into her third gin when a man sauntered over to shoot his shot.

"You're not John Wayne," she said, making herself laugh at the shoulder heavy way he walked. "Or are you?"

"Can be anything you want me to be, doll."

"Nice." She eyed him up and down. Under the scruff of

his unshaven face, was there a princely chin?

"How are you with stairs?" she asked.

"Wha?"

"Never mind. You got a name?"

"Patrick."

"Hmm. Patrick and Patricia. Up a tree. F-U-C-K-I-N-G. Nice ring to it."

"You're a wild one."

She leaned in. "You don't sniff as bad as you look. Come on. We'll go to mine."

His eyebrows shot up so fast she thought they'd fly right off his face. Before he hesitated, she lunged, planted a kiss on him so hard the barmaid dropped a glass that thumped to the floor without smashing.

When she released him, he sighed, blinked at her stupidly.

"I can do other stuff if you give me half the chance," she said. "Let's go, hot stuff."

It was a messy whirlwind when they stumbled through the door of the cottage. She kissed him, unlayered him, push him towards the stairs. Her passion flamed out.

"What you stopping for? Got me a rager going," he said, following her gaze. "Somebody up there?"

The shadow wasn't there. Maybe he never had been. She wished he was, though. But maybe Patrick could wrestle the tall stranger from her thoughts. Maybe Patrick was the type to settle down? A man of promises kept. Happy ever afters.

"Kiss me hard like that again," she said, doing her best kitten whisper the way men liked.

"You here on your own?"

"We gonna stand here with the dumb convo, or you wanna come upstairs and show me a few things?"

***

She sat up in bed gasping, clutching the covers to her naked chest. Her dream was a wide open sky that she tumbled through, no one in sight to help her fall.

The morning sun shone in through a small square of window, aching directly into her brain. She was alone with the smell of Patrick that wasn't so sweet. It stank like the inside of a rancid burp.

Patrick clattered about downstairs, swearing. A metal *psst* of a can of juice opening, then glugging noises like he swallowed half of it at once.

She leaned over, picked up her jeans, took something from a pocket. Patrick's wedding ring glinted in the bar of sun splaying over her bed. She wasn't sure why she'd reached over in the night, snuck it from his pocket to hers.

She held her hand out, placed the ring on her finger. "I am now Mrs…"

Mrs. what? He hadn't told her his surname.

The ring made a clink sound as she set it on the bedside table. She grabbed her robe, tied it tight, then lingered at the top of the stairs.

"Morning sweet buns," she said, joining Patrick in the messy kitchen. "Why so rushy? You're staying for breakfast, right?"

He didn't look at her, just went on chugging the can of juice before draining it, crinkling it up, setting it on the kitchen counter.

"Why don't you tell me all about yourself?" said Patricia, leaning on the counter. "Didn't tell me your last name amongst all that wild fun."

"And I won't be telling you, neither." A panic took over his face. He patted the pocket of his shirt, his jeans. "Think I lost something. Back in a sec."

"What you lost? Your wedding ring? Oh, get that look from your face. Think I'm daft?"

"Off my case, lady."

He walked by her, stinging the air with his deep sweat. She got up after him, giggling at the way he swaggered like a waddling pitbull.

"You know," she said, catching up to him, "I can do a lot more than she can. Do all the things. Keep you nice and cosy up in here. Plenty of space if you ever wanted to move in."

"You've got a screw loose, you have. Pure psycho talk."

The floorboards creaked as she marched toward him, reaching him at the doorway. "Just because my heart's bigger than the soulless witches about here, doesn't mean there's something wrong with me. Got a lot of love to give. Some lucky guy's gonna get all of it."

"Aye, good luck to him."

As he set his foot on the first stair, she imagined pushing him, snapping his leg beneath all that girth. The way the bone would snap as it bent in—

The gasp she sucked in was so loud it made Patrick stop, look back at her.

"You having a stroke there?" he said, shaking his head.

The man on the stairs was back.

He stood tall at the top of the staircase, sunlight dancing over him.

"You're the most beautiful thing I've seen my whole entire life," she muttered.

"You've got big problems and I'm having nought to do with it," said Patrick. "Get my ring and I'll be away. This never happened."

Her eyes roamed over the shadow man's features. He wasn't shadowy any more. The sharp angle of his chin. The green of his eyes. The tuftiness of his hair so thick she could run her hands through it. His green eyes sparkled. He was a dream.

He breathed. She could almost taste the scent of that breath. Almondy and sweet.

The ghost glared at Patrick as he shuffled his broad way up the stairs. When he settled his gem-bright eyes on her, she felt a heat crawl from the tips of her toes up the backs of her legs.

"I thought you'd left me," she said. "He... He doesn't deserve my love. It meant nothing."

"What you harping on about?" said Patrick. "You into meth or some shite? Where's that damn ring?"

She couldn't take her eyes from the statuesque figure as Patrick rummaged about in her bedroom.

"Ah, found you." Patrick appeared at the top of the

stairs, holding the ring, standing just behind the ghost. "Did you nick that off me last night?"

"You should go."

"Wouldn't stay around here with a headcase like you."

Her blood cringed, she stepped forward, clutching onto the banister. Patrick flowed through her ghost man as if he wasn't there. As if he wasn't the most perfect thing in existence.

Patrick stepped down, hissed out a cold giggle. "Did you hear me, you headcase? Absolute nut job. Psycho bit —"

The man pulsed forward, sending Patrick tumbling. She stepped back, slapping her hand over her mouth as Patrick twisted, hit the wall, his neck cracking into an unnatural angle.

He stopped at her feet, dead eyes accusing.

Shouldn't she feel bad for having watched a man die? Feel sick at the twisted bone sticking out the side of his neck?

The only thing coursing through her was unbridled elation. Her man had stepped out of the shadows and was walking down the stairs. A rising, fluttering sensation beat in her chest. She barely held on to the urge to fling herself at the man, squeeze him tight.

"Where have you been?" she asked, fumbling with the hem of her robe. Tears made her voice tremble. "Can't sleep when you're not here. I missed you something awful."

He cocked his head, examined her with sadness in his eyes. She knew then that he'd been hurt, too.

Her jaw clicked open as he lifted his hand, moved it slowly, ever so gently onto her cheek. It was as if she'd plunged herself into an ice-cold bath after a raging hot summer's day. The pleasure glowed inside, made her hold her breath.

He took his hand away, an apology in his eyes.

"No, no," she said. "Touch me again. I've... I've never felt that way before."

A curious smile tugged at his lips. Were those tears

running down his smooth face? When he went to touch her again, her insides almost begged for it.

His hand stopped in mid-air and he stared down at the dead body.

"We'll figure it out," she said, stepping back.

His eyes were ghostly fire that sent heat throbbing to her earlobes, her fingertips. How long did she spend gawking at him like a schoolgirl with her first crush?

He looked through the kitchen, to the window and the bright, undisturbed morning. A chuckle flowed from Patricia as she watched him set his feet apart, taking some imaginary tool into his hands, stabbing it into the carpet.

Her smile melted off her face when she saw he was digging. Her eyes went to the back window, to the garden. The place where they'd dug up a family of skeletons.

An ache crossed his features when he saw her expression. He was still so beautiful. Almost like chiselled stone.

"They didn't love you," she said, eyeing the garden. "You gave them everything you had and it still wasn't good enough." She reached out, took his hand. He felt almost as solid as a real person. Cold needled at her skin. Delicious, needy cold. "I'll give you everything I have. All of me."

His shoulders moved up and down, then he leaned forward, grabbed her into a hug. She tingled all over. Everywhere. When he kissed her on the forehead, she almost melted dead away. He sniffed so good. So pure.

When his lips moved, she heard his strong, sweet voice.

"You'll never leave me," he said. "Not ever?"

She stared down at Patrick. At the small trickle of blood hitting the step. Then she gazed back up at her tall ghost man. A man who would always be there. A man just for her.

No one had ever looked at her the way he did. She felt it in her toes.

Her happy ever after.

"I'll never leave you," she said. "Not ever. Now kiss me."

Lamia
Christian Dickinson

I feel the evening's air upon my skin;
The cold, stone floor beneath my well-wound tail.
The cavern's dankness pierces every scale;
I ope' the jar, and put my eyes back in.

Compelled by naught but vengeance' hunger keen,
To Corinth town I deftly make my way;
There grab a boy-child playing by the bay—
A prize most worthy of a Libyan Queen.

A youth of Corinth did my soul adore,
And for him did I make a wedding feast.
But that false teacher did my charms abhor,
And by his curse transformed me to a beast.
E'er since that day did I all love forsake,
And lure men solely for my thirst to slake.

This Cat Must Die!
Jason Lairamore

The heavy ceramic angel sitting high on the shelf above the sliding glass door was perfect for what Sham, the ethereal, had in mind. That fat orange cat had to die. Its death was the only way he could become a real ghost.

Late morning sun shining through the glass door warmed the tiled floor. That cursed cat, Cadmus, loved nothing more than to lie there to sleep.

Sham positioned the angel in just the right spot. At this distance from the floor, the force of the falling figurine should kill the cat easy. Then Cadmus could sleep forever.

Bwaahaahaahaa!

With that cat out of the way, Sham could get about doing what he was here to do: scare people. That's all he needed, just one little scare. That shouldn't be too hard. Maybe it wouldn't be ... this time.

He kept as silent and still as a statue as Cadmus pranced up to the inviting warm spot. It curled into a nice little ball, making a perfect, circular target. Sham, in a single fluid motion, toppled the angel from its precarious perch. He watched as the robed, winged angel fell, head over sandaled feet, directly toward his intended target. It was going to work! The figurine was falling in a path that would land it right in the center of Cadmus's extended head and neck.

CRASH! The sound of the shatter broke the near-absolute quiet of the room.

It had missed! How in all that was incorporeal had it missed?

But he didn't have time to ponder. Cadmus was up and coming for him. That heavy-bodied feline had already jumped from the tiled floor to the nearby tabletop. And it jumped again as soon as its feet were set.

Cadmus sailed toward him. Its teeth were out and its four claws were extended in his direction. All Sham could do was stare as true death came ever closer. He was about to be erased forever from the corporeal world. Cadmus's green eyes glinted fiercely, pinning Sham to his spot atop the high shelving as good as any witch's spell might have.

Sham smelt the animal stink waft ahead of the approaching beast. He felt the wind push at him as the claws that could rip his ethereal tissue to threads pierced the air just in front of where he floated.

Then the claws fell and embedded into the shelving. They raked gouges into the cheap, compressed wood as Cadmus's weight settled.

The cat's body swung, fully extended, below the edge of the creaking plank.

"MEOW – MEOW"

Cadmus was momentarily trapped.

"Cadmus! How could you?" wailed Jennifer. She was the female one of the two living in the house. "Mark! Come quick! Your cat just broke the antique my great aunt left us in her will."

"So that makes him my cat now?" Mark yelled from the other room. "What happened to Cadmus being our cat?"

Sham didn't bother to stay and find out who really owned the dreaded cat. He took his chance and fled for his afterlife.

He heard the washing machine running and thanked the kelpies above for the reprieve. He floated into the laundry room and settled himself in the corner where the wall met the roof. Cadmus wouldn't come in there. The cat was scared to near hysteria when it came to washing machines.

As his aura settled to a less frizzy, wave-like ambience, he thought of his next move. Time was running out. He had to get rid of that cat before the sun set. Ghosts couldn't live where a cat lived. That was one of the rules. And with his testing in just a few hours, he'd be disqualified if the ghost judges found out there was a housecat living here. He couldn't be disqualified, not again. This was his last chance. He had run out of appeals. He had to pass his final ghost test tonight.

He had it!

He floated from the laundry room and into the den. Mark and Jennifer were watching television. He saw no sign of Cadmus. Perhaps the cat was back to sleeping in the sun. Or, maybe it had gotten in trouble enough that it was lying low under one of the beds.

He made his slow way to the kitchen. On the stove was a large cast iron skillet and in that skillet was bacon grease. Cadmus had been going crazy over that bacon this morning. That grease would make the perfect bait.

After careful inspection that Cadmus wasn't hiding somewhere nearby, he descended down to the stovetop. The grease in the pan had hardened to a nasty, gritty white. The dirty spoons were in the sink. He grabbed the smallest metal one and skimmed low over the countertop back to the pan on the stove. He got a good dollop of his bait and left the kitchen, skirted the den, and entered the hallway.

The room at the end of hall was the place where the male one, Mark, painted. He had a drafting table and a few canvases set up. Sham stuck the end of the spoon in an open electric plug. A slight buzz told him he had made good contact. The gray grease in the spoon started to melt. He floated to the nearest canvas and hid behind it to wait.

The cat came trotting to the room as if on cue. Sham could not have asked for better timing. This was going to work!

Cadmus darted to the spoon like a younger, skinnier, version of itself. When it got near to the spoon it slowed. For an instant Sham thought that Cadmus had caught on to the trap, but no, it was just doing was all cats do. It sniffed around the edges before fully committing to the treat.

One of Cadmus's whiskers got too close. An arc of blue fire shot from the spoon to the cat's nose. A shriek echoed off the walls as Cadmus leaped away. The spoon was dislodged from the socket. All of Sham's collected grease dribbled into the carpet. He looked to Cadmus, hoping the leap had been nothing but a final death throe, but such wasn't the case. Cadmus crouched, its feet tucked neatly under it. It tongue licked at the smoldering end of a burnt whisker. The cat's eyes were a glaring green intensity directed right at him.

AAAAHHHHHHH!

He screamed and floated away as Cadmus leaped to the canvas he was hiding behind. The cat shredded the canvas with one good tug of it claws. It leaped again, to the next canvas, ripping it too as it tried to get to Sham.

For his part, Sham floated faster than he thought possible. But, he knew it was no use. The cat, by instinct or plain dumb happenstance, had positioned itself to effectively block the door, Sham's only way out.

Cadmus hopped to the drafting table and crouch-walked up to its highest point. Sham took refuge in the far, upper corner of the room, but it was no good. Cadmus could make the jump.

Cadmus seemed to know it had won as well. It took its time. It crouched low in preparation to spring. Its eyes were wide, its pupils dilated.

Mark came barging in. He took one look at the situation and grabbed Cadmus by the scruff. With a single heave he tossed the heavy-bodied cat to the hall.

"Jennifer, get your cat!" Mark called as he eyed the damage Cadmus had made. "He has ruined every one of my projects back here. What has gotten into that cat today?"

"Maybe he needs more attention," Jennifer called back.

"And why does it smell like bacon in here?" Mark added.

"What?"

Sham slipped past the furious Mark and sought refuge in a less hostile environment. He needed time to think, and to once again calm down. For the second time in one day, he had almost died true.

He ventured in a shocked haze to the master bedroom. He usually didn't spend much time in there. The live ones slept there. And since he was forbidden to scare the living unless properly supervised or until he passed his sanctioned ghost testing, he tried to stay away from the temptation.

But, there was a vaulted ceiling in there, and it was high enough for his fear of Cadmus to go away.

He floated a circle around the shaft of the ceiling fan while he fretted over his dilemma. For the umpteenth time, he cursed selecting this house as the site for his testing. But what was he supposed to do? He had been left with little choice. This house was one of the new ones. The other incorporeal beings hadn't scoped it out yet. So, naturally he had jumped on it, had registered it and everything, just to keep the others away. How was he to know that the living beings owned a housecat? He had not had the time to check it out properly. No spirit had.

It had been the last house available that met specs for his testing, though. And there was no telling how long it would be before another came up. However long was too long. He was tired of failing over and over again. He was going to pass the test tonight. It was such a simple test. All the ghosts said so. All he had to do was scare somebody.

If only he could get that cat out of the house. Outside cats were okay. Maybe he'd been going about this all wrong. He didn't necessarily have to kill the cat. It just couldn't be there during the short amount of time it took for him to pass his test.

He waited till the 6 o'clock news came on before slipping from the master bedroom and into the hall. The sun was starting to set. It was now or never. He had one shot at this.

"See, Mark," Jennifer said from the den, "all Cadmus needed was a little cuddle time."

Sham froze at the end of the hall.

"Yeah, looks like," Mark said.

"Cadmus has already taught us so much about caring for a little one," Jennifer added.

"You're going to be a good dad," she said.

"Not as good as you're going to be a mom."

Sham couldn't wait any longer. The sun had already

turned from yellow to orange in its descent.

He eased around the corner and looked down onto the den.

The two living sat on the couch. They had their faces smashed together. Cadmus, sitting between them, had its head turned up. Its piercing green eyes had already found Sham.

BOO? Sham's voice was more a whimper than anything remotely scary.

"MEOWRR", Cadmus growled deep in its throat. Sham started his shaky way across the ceiling.

Cadmus jumped to Mark's lap and then vaulted up toward Sham.

"HEY!" Mark yelled. "Easy with the claws, Cadmus."

The cat didn't come anywhere near high enough to threaten Sham, but still Sham shrank away. With a glance to the ever setting sun, he forced himself to stay in the room. This wouldn't work unless the two living saw it.

BOOOOO - he taunted the cat as loud as he could manage while he slid along the ceiling back and forth.

"MEOWRR, FITT FITT," Cadmus growled. It jumped over and over up toward him, never coming close, but always coming near enough to almost scare the shade out of him.

"What's wrong with Cadmus?" Jennifer asked. Mark didn't answer.

BOOOOO – Sham kept at it. The sun was nearly down. He got more brazen in his attempts, reckless even. He hovered above the television. Cadmus jumped up atop the entertainment center and launched itself at him. Sham floated toward the couch. He wanted Cadmus to hit the live ones.

But he had underestimated the cat's speed. Cadmus was coming. The height of the entertainment center had giving it all the added altitude it needed to reach him. Cadmus was going to hit him and there was nothing he could do about it.

His attention was so fixed on his advancing death that he had not noticed that Mark had stood from the couch.

He bounced from the living one's outstretched hand.

Mark caught Cadmus in midair right in from of Sham's ethereal face.

"MIERRR," Cadmus growled as it twisted in Mark's grip. Sham dropped down and floated away as the angry feline tried in vain to reach him.

Mark opened the door to the outside and tossed Cadmus into the yard.

Yes! It had worked!

"Mark?" Jennifer asked. "You threw Cadmus outside. How are we going to be good parents if you throw Cadmus outside when he's having a tantrum? We can't throw our baby outside if it's crying, you know."

Mark grabbed Jennifer by the hand and brought her to her feet. "Babies have tantrums - cats don't, not at nothing anyway."

"What?"

"There is something else here."

She looked around, her eyes passing right through Sham. Of course she couldn't see him. Only real ghosts and the higher-ups had the power to make themselves visible.

"Come with me," Mark said. He led her from the room and into the hall. Sham went to follow when three ghosts slipped through the wall and into the room.

"Honored sirs," he said at once. He had been through this so many times that he knew the drill by rote.

"Ethereal Sham, we have arrived at the appointed time and in the proper frame to witness your final appeal for acceptance into the Guild of Ghosts."

Sham couldn't tell which of the three had spoken. They had each arrived as floating white orbs, the official frame for testing.

"Thank you for the chance," Sham said with a bow. "I'll not let you down."

He had added the sentiment on purpose. It was unneeded and probably not worth the specter air he'd spent to say it, but this was his last chance. He might as well say what he wished.

"This is a waste of time," one said, "just like the other times."

Sham fought hard to keep his aura in check.

"Why does it smell of cat in here?" another asked.

"An outside cat is all," Sham said, pointing to the window. Cadmus was on the outside window ledge MEOWING its fool head off.

"You are lucky to have found a suitable house at all," a ghost said. "Domestic cat breeding has really gotten out of hand in today's age."

"A review of the rules then," one ghost said.

"As if he needs reminding," another said.

"He has attempted this trial more times than any spirit in the realm – and still, nothing."

"When will he learn that some spirits aren't made to scare?"

"Excuse me," Sham interrupted. He hated how they talked about him as if weren't there. "You mentioned the rules..."

"Yes, quickly then. We will grant you the power to reveal yourself, but you may do so for only a fraction of time and only in the peripheral of a living one's vision. Do you remember the list of acceptable noises and motions?"

"I am well aware," Sham said flatly. Mark and Jennifer would be back any time. He would show them what he could do. He'd pass this test in a flash.

"Normal sounds are fine – knocks, thuds, creaks. Some laughter and whispers and the like are acceptable within a very fine range."

"I know the limits of the test," Sham said. "Thank you."

He could hear Mark and Jennifer returning as they walked the hall back toward the kitchen and den. As soon as they entered, he went into action. He used the powers granted him by the council for just this purpose. The powers were a parody of what real Ghosts could do, but still. Even those small added abilities let Sham know that all the humiliation he had taken over the years was worth it.

He placed horrific visions at the corner of their vision.

He caused a few of the cabinet doors to creak. He cackled a bit in their ears. He needed their attention so that he might truly frighten them. He blew a little cold, dead air in their faces then turned the television off and back on. None of it worked. They walked on, straight to the kitchen table.

He pulled out his ace. Jennifer and Mark had been talking about having a baby since the first time he'd seen them. He gave them the sound of a distant thump and followed that with a baby's cry. Surely, that would get Jennifer's attention.

But no, they both had their attention focused on the items in their hands.

"Are you sure about this Mark?" Jennifer asked. "I heard that stuff was real. You could bring a demon over to this side."

"You bet it's real," Mark answered.

"I say," one of the ghosts popped up, breaking protocol. The ghost judges were supposed to remain silent during testing. "Is that what I think it is?"

"My great grandfather gave this to me," Mark said.

"That is what you think it is," another of the ghosts added. "A Ouija board is being prepared."

"But why must I use my candle holders?" Jennifer asked in a whine. "They were my mother's favorite. 'Glass from the old country' she says."

"They are old," Mark said. "Old is important. And you care about them. That will make this work better."

Sham had stopped trying to spook them. He stared in horror as his last and only chance at Ghosthood went up in specter smoke.

"Why are they attempting a connection now?" one of the orbs asked suspiciously.

"What have you done?" another cried.

"Only a true ghost can resist the Ouija call."

Jennifer lit the candles while Mark killed the lights.

"You will betray our presence, Sham," a ghost wailed. "Do you know the damage you might cause?"

"We will have to consult with the Witches to get this

fixed."

"We hate dealing with the Witches, half in – half out ... and their blasted, black cats, never knowing if they are going to kill you true."

Sham could feel the pull of the board even as they spoke. When Jennifer and Mark put their fingers to the pointer he floated in that direction.

"Blast you, Sham," one of the ghosts cursed. "I will see you staked to the light for this, mark my words!"

"Spirit," Mark said. He was talking directly to Sham. The feeling was surreal.

"Come to us and speak," Mark continued.

Sham came closer as bidden. He could not stop himself.

The orbs still floated, watching. They were bound to stay for the time of his testing.

Though compelled to obey, Sham did turn his eyes enough to catch their glowing presence. Was this how his dreams were to end, him making a complete fool out of himself, being used by a couple of live beings?

No. He would not go out like this. He struggled as he floated ever closer to the pair of living hands that lightly touched the Ouija pointer.

He passed close to one of the candles. Using every bit of power he had, he pushed the candle until it began to topple.

"My candle," Jennifer screamed. She tore her hand from the pointer and grabbed for the heirloom.

"My board," Mark's excitement echoed Jennifer's own. He jerked the board away from the descending fire.

Sham continued toward the table, carried as he was by the original force of the Ouija board. When he reached the tabletop he experienced a most odd sensation. The table felt pliable. It felt soft. Before he knew it he was passing through it. The taste of cleaning oil and wood pressed tight against him.

How had he done that? Only the true Ghosts or higher ups could pass through the physical.

He turned his attention to the three orbs floating nearby.

"The living beings were frightened. You passed the trial," one said.

"They were fearful for the safety of their possessions," another said.

"You are one lucky spook."

Sham rose to once again float through the table. Mark and Jennifer were re-setting the board, but he no longer felt the pull he had moments ago.

He'd won! He had passed the final test!

"Welcome to the Ghosthood," a ghost said.

He glanced around the darkened room and tried to memorize the moment. This was where his dream had come true. He was finally a member of the Ghosthood. On the window ledge outside, Cadmus continued to meow. It eyed Sham with a green-eyed focus that only a cat could achieve. Sham, though he shivered at the intensity directed his way, smiled.

He had won.

The Hungry House
Randall Andrews

We thought our voodoo magic hadn't worked,
that in the course of the casting, the fickle winds of fate—
so difficult to tame—had shifted and spoiled the spell.

We left the doll lie, glass eyes open wide
to the sky, and gathering our tools
and talismans, we headed into the house . . .
disappointed.

The words of our incantation were echoing in my ears:
"Have anger, have hunger, have rapture, have strife,
have life!"

I was startled by the sound of the door
slamming closed of its own accord,
and the click of the lock that followed.
It was then that I realized our magic *had* worked,
and my partners and I had been swallowed.

Underworld
Paul Lonardo

When Thomas Couchon first saw the ghost, he was not as startled as he thought he would have been by such a sight. He had arrived at the midtown Manhattan restaurant early, wanting to relax with a few drinks before Jerry Preciado and a couple other Coda Pharmaceuticals reps showed up to meet him. Over the course of the next hour that he had been waiting at the bar, Thomas put away three scotch and waters while the ghost polished off a three-course meal and had started on the pasta dish, a heaping bowl of spaghetti and meatballs.

The alcohol went down much too easily, and Thomas was feeling the effects. The lightheadedness alone could not fully explain the vision at the back of the restaurant; he knew there had to be more to it.

He took a deep breath and cleared his head of everything before looking back over in that direction, but he could still see it. The figure was dining alone in a back booth. The only illumination came from the flame of a single flickering candle in the middle of the table. The diner's girth was such that the meager candlelight was not sufficient to cast its glow across both mighty shoulders at the same time. As a frequent purchaser of fine men's wear himself, Thomas guessed that, in the living years, the dead man's tailoring fees would have been every bit as costly as the well-made pinstripe suit itself. The brim of a black-banded white fedora that the specter wore was angled downward sufficiently to conceal its face. The plate now contained only excess tomato sauce, which the apparition sopped up with thick slices of Italian bread.

Slowly, the dead man lifted his massive head and raised one meaty hand off the table, jabbing his index finger at Thomas, as if trying to alert him to something. Thomas shuddered inwardly and quickly turned away.

You know you've had too much to drink, farm boy, Thomas told himself, *when you start seeing fat guys who aren't there eating spaghetti and beckoning you.*

He knew it wasn't real because no one else in the restaurant so much as glanced over at that closed section of the dining room the entire time. And no waitress ever went over to serve the food. The dishes that the ghost ate just appeared, and from what Thomas could tell, none of them were even on the menu, including the shrimp and scungilli salad that the ghost started to eat next.

Thomas checked his watch; it was almost nine o'clock. Jerry would be along any minute. He raised his glass to his mouth and took a long swallow, keeping it pressed against his lips until the scotch was drained. As soon as the empty snifter touched the polished walnut surface of the bar top, the bartender removed it and replaced it with a fresh drink. Thomas nodded his appreciation to the elderly man behind the bar. He was not looking forward to the reunion with his old college frat brother, whom he never liked. Jerry never took anything seriously, and he was always joking around.

There were other things about Jerry that rubbed Thomas the wrong way, particularly the history Brooke had with Jerry, but he didn't like to think about that. He was battling his own demons, which were going to tear his marriage to pieces if he didn't do something about it.

Still, Thomas doubted that Jerry could have changed much in that time, and how it came to be that Jerry was the purchasing agent for Coda Pharmaceuticals while Thomas was a salesman peddling chromatography instrumentation to the company was too much of a coincidence. From the start, Thomas was troubled by the idea of having to fly all the way to New York to work with Jerry, but here he was.

Thomas found solace thinking how he would be home with his wife and young son in a few short days. The prospect of being back in a familiar, comfortable environment buoyed his mood. In this contented state of mind, when he looked up, he fully expected the vision to have returned to the bottom of his glass where it came from. However, not only was the ghost still there, but it was peering directly at him. The dim glow from the candle cast shadows making the scowl on its face even more ominous. The white cloth napkin tucked in the shirt collar and draped down across its chest was splattered with pasta sauce. For a second time, the ghost raised its arm and beckoned at Thomas, only more urgently than before.

Thomas averted his eyes, looking up at the baseball game on the television above the bar. The Yankees were playing some team whose uniform he didn't recognize. He hadn't followed baseball in any meaningful way since he was a kid, and even then, as a boy who worked the family wheat farm, baseball wasn't a priority.

The bartender, who would glance up to check the score periodically as he went about his duties, noticed him watching and made a comment about the opposing pitcher being a "stud." Thomas nodded in agreement, pretending to be interested in the play-by-play.

Though the dining room was three-quarters full, the bar was practically empty. Two guys in their mid-twenties were seated directly across the horseshoe-shaped bar from Thomas. They were talking to a red-headed waitress who was off-duty and sipping a glass of white wine. They were in their own bubble, flirting and laughing, unaware of everything that was going on around them. The only other person at the bar was a guy seated a couple stools away on Thomas' left. The man's profile revealed a considerable amount of information; bulky, middle-aged, with dark hair neatly swept back, coolly nursing a cocktail. He was wearing a charcoal gray suit and an old-fashioned pocket-watch, the chain clearly visible in his vest pocket. He had a polka dot handkerchief in the jacket pocket and an expensive cashmere scarf around his neck. There was a long white trench coat draped on the back of his chair and a Russian-style fur hat on the top of the bar between him and Thomas.

Thomas could not recall seeing the man sitting there when he entered the bar an hour earlier, nor had he observed anyone come in during that time. He figured that the man arrived when he was distracted with the baseball game.

As the man unwrapped a fat cigar and stuck it between his lips, he turned slightly to his left and glanced in the direction of the feasting ghost. The man suddenly raised his left hand, which was sporting a gold pinky ring, and pointed back across his body at Thomas without looking at him. It was an inquisitory gesture that asked, *Him?*

Just then Thomas felt a hand clamp down on his shoulder and he flinched. He abruptly stood and turned around, hearing the laughing bray of Jerry Preciado before he saw him.

"Tom Boy," Jerry said with jaunty exuberance.

"Jerry Preciado," Thomas responded, manufacturing a good-humored smile.

"I'll be damned! My Washington State University, Alpha Tau Omega, brother! How long has it been, Tom Boy? Five years? You haven't changed a bit."

"If I didn't know you any better, I might take that as a compliment," Thomas said.

Jerry feigned indignation and said, "Can't a guy make an innocent remark to old college buddy without being suspected of anything?"

"Most guys could. But unless I'm mistaken, you were the one who put knock-out drops in Stephen Rogers beer and tied him naked to the flagpole in the quad during finals."

Jerry laughed heartily at the memory. "That was funny, now that you mention it. Not very original, but damn funny. At least at the time, it was. God, I haven't thought about that in years." He shook his head wistfully. "Stephen Rogers...Was he a loser, or what? But like I said, it's been a long time. So much has changed. I've changed, believe it or not. I don't do those kinds of things anymore."

Thomas nodded, his smile never faltering. It didn't appear to him that Jerry had changed in the least. Not a single blonde hair was out of place, complexion tanned and unblemished, and he was dressed in a business casual style that would have been appropriate in either the boardroom or on a yacht. And he was still an unapologetic asshole.

"Some coincidence, huh, Tom Boy?"

"What's that?"

"Who would have guessed that we'd meet again this way? Me, a budgeting executive for an upstart pharmaceutical firm. and you selling instrumentation to me?"

Thomas nodded. "I was thinking the same thing."

Jerry held his arms out to either side in a welcoming gesture. "It's really good to see you, Tom Boy. Put her there."

When Jerry extended his right hand, Thomas almost expected him to be hiding one of those joy buzzers in his palm as a practical joke. It turned out to be the standard grab-and-two-pull handshake.

"Ryan. Sam," Jerry called out.

The two twenty-somethings across the bar looked up. One waved in acknowledgment and then headed over. The other took a moment to remove a business card from his wallet, write his cell phone number on the back, and hand it to the redhead before walking around the bar to join his friend. Neither of them glanced at the man seated near Thomas. One of them even walked into the man's arm as he passed without so much as an apology. To Thomas, it seemed more like he had walked *through* the man's arm. The man just sat there chewing on the end of his unlit cigar.

"This is Ryan Landry," Jerry said, nodding toward the first one who'd made his way over to them. "And Sam Perry. Two bums I work with. Say hello to Tommy Raymer." The men exchanged handshakes. "Tom and I went to college together. We were in the same fraternity."

"Weren't you president of the frat?" Ryan asked Jerry.

"I was co-president my senior year," Jerry acknowledged. "Tom Boy here is from Idaho. Hey, what's the name of that town you're from again? Bumfuck?"

Jerry hadn't wasted any time diving into the country bumpkin jokes, Thomas thought. The clown prince of the Alpha Tau Omega house was just getting warmed up, and now he had his sights set on one of his favorite targets.

"Boomstack," Thomas corrected him.

Jerry slapped him on the back and laughed. "I'm just screwing with you, Tom Boy."

Thomas grinned, maintaining a guarded disposition. So far, Jerry showed no signs of seeing the ghost, and for the first time, Thomas began to wonder if perhaps Jerry knew more about it than he was letting on. It was not implausible that Jerry had arranged to have this meeting at a familiar restaurant where he could set up a prank whose only purpose was to humiliate a college frat brother he hadn't seen in five years. In fact, it was highly probable, Thomas thought.

"Tom Boy...HEY, TOM BOY!"

"Huh?" Thomas had momentarily tuned out the conversation that Jerry and his associates were having.

"I said, what are you drinking, Tom Boy?"

"Ahhh," Thomas stammered, mopping his damp forehead with the palm of his hand. He was suddenly feeling very warm. "I'm good," he finally said.

"What?" Jerry feigned surprise. "Do my ears deceive me? As I recall, at our frat parties, nobody could keep up with you. WSU should have given that liver of yours an honorary degree for all the work it did during those four years."

"I really just want to get to my hotel room, call my wife, and unwind. I'm beat. It was a long flight."

Jerry draped an arm across Thomas' shoulders. "Oh, hey, how's Brooke doing, anyway?" he asked, his eyes now wide and his smile morphing into a smirk.

Thomas faltered. "She's real good."

"Say hello for me. Tell her I was asking about her." Jerry looked over at Ryan and Sam.

"Brooke and I dated for while in college," he told them. "That was before Tom Boy here stole her away from me. Ain't that right, Tom Boy?" he asked, turning back to Thomas and pulling their shoulders together.

The two other men exchanged a furtive look, as if they knew something Thomas didn't.

Sure, Thomas thought. *Jerry probably told them all kinds of intimate details about the time that he and Brooke were together.*

"Carl, I'll have the usual," Jerry shouted out to the bartender. "And get these jokers whatever they want."

Ryan and Sam bellied up to the bar and Jerry sat down in the chair between Thomas and the cigar-chomping stranger.

"You have a kid now, don't you, Tom Boy?" Jerry asked. "I thought I saw something on social media a while back."

Thomas smiled. "Nolan."

"That's great. How old is he?"

"He's six."

"Six, huh. Well, say hello to your wife *and* my son." Jerry cackled and pulled away from Thomas, giving him a playful punch in the gut.

Thomas just wanted to get out of there.

"Tell you what, Tom Boy," Jerry began. "This is as much a reunion as it is a business meeting, so why don't we get a table, have nice dinner, a few cocktails, get caught up, talk some shop, and Coda will pay for everything. What do you say? I picked this restaurant specifically with you in mind, Tom Boy. You'll love it. I eat here at least twice a week. Everything on the menu fantastic, but if Rena's is known for anything, it's that it has the best steak in the city. A beef-fed Idaho boy like you should appreciate that." He patted Thomas' belly-bulge and laughed. "Seriously, people come here from all around the world for their filet mignon. No shit, Tom Boy. I wouldn't lie to you."

Jerry was on a roll now. He was talking so fast that the words seemed to escape his lips before they were fully formed.

"And if it's atmosphere you prefer, look no further," Jerry continued. "There are plenty of people in here right now who will swear to you that they believe this building is haunted by the vengeful spirit of Louie 'Black Shoes' Salivucci, an up-and-coming soldier with one of the notorious New York crime families, who was gunned down in this very room sometime back in the 1940's."

The statement nailed Thomas' feet to the floor. Despite his distrust of anything that came out of Jerry's mouth, he found himself being drawn into the story about the mob killing. He had always been fascinated with organized crime and its history of grisly murders. He had read every book on the subject that he could get his hands on. The mobster-on-mobster assassinations held a special allure because of their shocking brutality, none more so than any of the notorious execution-style slayings that have been carried out in public. The crime scene photos were etched in his mind from the long list of gangland shootings that include Giuseppe "Joe the Boss" Masseria, Earl "Hymie" Weiss, Arthur "Dutch Schultz" Flegenheimer, Charles "Cherry Nose" Gioe, Tommy Bilotti, Frankie Yale, Antonio "Tony the Scourge" Lombardo, Jack "Machine Gun Jack" McGurn, Albert "The Mad Hatter" Anastasia, Camillo "Carmine" "The Cigar" Galante, Paul "Big Paul" Castellano, and particularly Angelo "The Docile Don" Bruno, who had been killed by a single gunshot blast to the back of the head as he sat in his car. At that time, crime families were forbidden from getting involved in narcotic distribution, but Bruno ignored the edict and made a bundle in the heroin market. Bruno's body was found with dollar bills stuffed in his mouth and in his anus to symbolize his wanton greed.

Jerry knew all about Thomas' perverse preoccupation with underworld violence. His frat room had been literally wallpapered with movie posters from such classic films as *Little Caesar, White Heat,* and *The Public Enemy,* as well as the more violent modern mobster movies like *Scarface, Goodfellas,* and *The Departed.*

Gangsters, with their dual nature of family commitment and moral corruption, and the hypocrisy of their code of ethics, held as much interest to Thomas now as ever, and he figured that Jerry had to be banking on this fixation to set up this practical joke.

Thomas had to admit that it was genius, far exceeding any of the hijinks and college pranks that Jerry would typically pull.

"This used to be an Italian restaurant," Jerry continued. "One that was notorious for catering to a mob clientèle. As the story goes, Salivucci was seated in the back of the restaurant, dining with his mistress. His back was to the wall, as always, ever on the lookout for assassins. He never expected his demise to come the way it did, however, in a mob restaurant run by his own cousin."

Thomas absorbed every detail of Jerry's account, recreating the scene in his mind. He couldn't help picturing Carmine Galante eating lunch outside on the open patio of the Brooklyn restaurant owned by his cousin when three masked men burst in on the mobster and his two bodyguards, shooting Galante to death. Two others had been killed alongside Galante, but the bodyguards, who had done nothing to protect their boss, were left unharmed. The unknown gunmen then ran out of the restaurant. There was a famous picture taken of the crime scene afterward showing Galante's corpse lying in a pool of blood with his left eye shot out and his cigar still clenched in his mouth.

"Salivucci had a bodyguard with him that night," Jerry said, right on cue. "But Black Shoes wanted to be alone with his lady. While the goon went to the lounge to get tanked, talking to a couple of prostitutes, Salivucci's *goomah* excused herself to go powder her nose. The mobster was left alone to finish his double order of spaghetti and meatballs. Just then, the waiter, some young kid, came by with the check. Salivucci angrily told him to get lost and come back when he was finished eating. But the kid just stood there, calm as can be, staring at the irate gangster who had pasta sauce dripping down his chin. Then the waiter leaned in close to old Black Shoes and said, 'The bill's come due.'" Jerry's pronounced the words that the waiter was purported to have spoken in a deliberate and ominous tone.

Thomas sat mesmerized, listening intently to every detail Jerry offered.

"At that point, Salivucci knew, but it was too late." Jerry paused for dramatic effect, then the cadence of his voice quickened and sharpened. "He started to get up as the waiter pulled a sawed-off shotgun out from behind his back. He quickly fired point blank and took the guinea hood's face off like a Halloween mask, neat as you please."

Thomas flinched inwardly. He could hear the percussion of the blast in his head.

Before finishing his narrative, Jerry took a sip from a glass of some clear alcohol that Thomas had not seen Carl bring over. "Salivucci's mistress and his bodyguard - who had never gotten up off the bar stool - were both rumored to be in on planning the hit. The waiter who pulled the trigger had been brought in from Italy so nobody would recognize him. Some believe he went back to the old country never to be heard from again. Others say he became a capo with one of the New York families, I forget which one. According to some accounts, the shooter was bold enough to lift a C-note out of Salivucci's wallet as a tip before he left, if you can believe that." Jerry let out an exhaustive breath and stared back at Thomas.

"That's quite a story," Thomas said.

"Sure is," Jerry agreed. "But there's more." He took another sip of his drink, savoring it on his tongue before swallowing. "Today, there are some people who claim to have seen the ghost of Louie Salivucci sitting in the back of the bar, eating his trademark double order of spaghetti and meatballs."

Jerry had to be making it all up, Thomas thought. As intriguing as the tale had been, Thomas had never heard of Black Shoes Salivucci or the slaying. Now, he had to decide how he was going to play this. And quickly. The way he saw it, he had only two choices. One was to let Jerry off the hook and confess that he knew all about his high-tech prank, or two, pretend he didn't see anything and bide his time until the gag stretched itself beyond the point of being funny and then spring it on Jerry that he had been wise to him all along. Thomas opted for the latter, and the more he thought about how the elaborate hoax was going to blow up in Jerry's face, the better Thomas felt about the whole thing.

Thomas suddenly realized that the other Coda employees must be in on it too, along with everyone else in the bar. They were all sitting back waiting for him to start ranting about the ghost so they could point and laugh at the dumb rube from Idaho known as Tom Boy in his college fraternity, and whose wife used to date Jerry when they were all attending Washington State University together.

Thomas' painted-on smile began to chip away, replaced by bitter anger and rage. He wondered why someone he hadn't seen in so long would go this far to demean and embarrass him.

"All right, Tom Boy," Jerry resigned. "You win. I thought I could convince you to stay after telling you that story. I tried. Oh, well. Only one thing left to tell you." He jerked his head back over his left shoulder at the secluded table at the back of the bar. "It's beyond the far corner of the bar. All the way in the back. You can't miss it."

"What?" Thomas was so surprised his voice cracked.

"The head," Jerry replied. "When we first got here, I couldn't help notice the way your eyes were darting around looking for the restrooms. You may as well empty the old bladder before you leave."

"Good idea," Thomas said, getting to his feet. "I'll be right back."

Thomas was determined not to give the gangland phantom a second look when he passed by it on the way to the men's room. He did not want to give Jerry the satisfaction. He couldn't resist a passing glance, however, and what he saw out of the corner of his eye almost stopped him in his tracks. He managed to keep moving, despite the grisly scene that was now on display at the back of the restaurant. The would-be don who had been sitting alone in the booth had no face to speak of, though his fedora somehow maintained its position, albeit slightly askew, atop the shattered remains of his skull. The wall behind him was splashed with blood and bone fragments. More gore dripped from the unsightly wound, puddling on top of the remaining spaghetti in the bowl like grotesque tomato sauce.

Although Thomas could not be exactly sure how this stunt had been engineered, the creation of the mobster-ghost was ingenious. He really had to hand it to Jerry this time, abandoning the old standby red neck and inbreeding jokes for a bit of 21st century techno-wizardry. Louie "Black Shoes" Salivucci could only have been the product of a uniquely talented, if somewhat deranged, special effects make-up magician.

Thomas's own head swooned at the mere sight of it. If he had to look at the leaking remains of the prosthetic head a moment longer than he did, he was sure he would have gotten sick to his stomach right then and there. He only hoped that any incidental facial expression or physical reaction he had to the tableau went undetected by Jerry or anyone else who might be watching him at that moment.

As Thomas gripped the edge of the sink in the men's room and waited for the nausea to pass, he was suddenly struck with the notion that there might be a video camera aimed at him at that very moment, ready to record even his most subtle gasp of horror for the pranksters to laugh about for hours afterward. Thomas wouldn't put it past Jerry, so he straightened up and looked at his reflection in the mirror. He saw the terror evident on his pallid face and in the cast of his eyes, and he tried to will it away.

Just then the bathroom door opened and the stranger seated near him at the bar entered, stopping just far enough inside to allow the door to close behind him. The wide lapels of his tapered jacket made them look even larger and more threatening. He reached back and slid the dead bolt across the door jamb. As if the lock and the catch were made of cotton, this action produced no sound.

The man turned back and stood silently facing Thomas. He showed no sign of hostility, though his expression was unreadable as stone.

"What do you want?" Thomas asked the brute, his voice quavering.

When the man did not respond right away, Thomas

became gravely concerned. Suddenly the man reached behind his back and produced something short and black. It took Thomas a moment to recognize the object. It was a sawed-off, double-barreled shotgun.

"What's that for?" Again, his inquiry was ignored.

The man raised the weapon, chest-level, and Thomas cringed. He expected to first feel the mule kick of the impact on his torso, and then hear the sound of his warm insides spilling out onto the cold ceramic title. But the man spun the weapon around in his palm and offered the handle to Thomas, who found himself reaching for it without being told. Then he tucked it in his belt in the small of his back, concealing it under his coat.

"The bill's come due," the man finally said, then turned and threw back the silent bolt before walking out of the bathroom.

Alone again, Thomas paused a moment to reflect on what just transpired. He could hear his heart beating in his chest and he was sweating profusely. Bending over the sink, he splashed cold water on his face, hoping it might clear his head a little.

Then it occurred to him.

Of course, he thought. *This was all part of the charade. Jerry had sent the man in with the shotgun to see what he would do.*

Thomas almost laughed out loud. Reminding himself about the possibility of a hidden camera, he quickly patted his face dry with a paper towel and went back out to the bar. He was more determined than ever not to mention a word to Jerry about the slain Salivucci, or the man that had approached him in the bathroom with the shotgun. The longer he held off, Thomas told himself, the more sour the taste of Jerry's own medicine would be to him.

He lied to Jerry, telling him how great it was to see him and apologized to all three of them for cutting out early. He said he would see them at the Coda plant in the morning and left the restaurant, taking a taxi back to his hotel. The filth and noise of the city gave him a headache. He needed a drink, but he bypassed the mini bar and the first thing he did when he got to his room was call Brooke. She sounded surprised to hear his voice.

"Why are calling?" she asked.

"What do you mean, Brooke?"

"Tom, don't do this."

"Do what? Can't I talk to my family? Put Ethan on the phone."

"He's sleeping. Do you know what time it is?"

Thomas sighed. The protracted silence that rang in his ears filled him with anger. "I saw Jerry tonight," he spat. "As if you didn't know."

"Jerry?"

"Jerry Preciado. I'm sure you remember him."

"Oh, God! You're not going to start on that again. I don't know why you're so obsessed with him."

"Obsessed! Me? You're the one who slept with him, for Christ's sake!"

"You're drunk, aren't you?"

"I only had a few cocktails. It was business."

"You broke your promise. Again."

Thomas gripped the phone tightly and steadied his voice. "I need to come home."

"We've been all though this."

"I'll go back into treatment. Give me another chance. I'm sorry, Brooke. Let me come home. Please."

She began to sob. "It's too late, Tom," she said, her voice trembling. "You still don't get it. I can't have you around Ethan. I don't trust you. You need help. I can't do this anymore. It's over. Goodnight."

"Wait, Brooke. I love you." But she already hung up. He immediately redialed, but she didn't pick up. His call went right to voice mail and he knew she had turned her phone off. The pain would have been unbearable if he hadn't known how to suppress it. He invaded the mini bar, even though that alone didn't do much good. He didn't want to feel *anything*. He didn't want to think about his failure as a husband and a father. To achieve this, his mind had to cover up the reality, block out everything and pretend that his life was fine. Others might see through this farce, but he was the only one who had to believe the lie. This was something he had become very skilled at over time.

In the morning, he wanted to call Brooke, but he had overslept. With the little time he had available, he spent getting himself ready to face the world. He reeked of alcohol. He had always been able to mask his drinking effectively from the people he worked with by adhering to a strict regimen of personal hygiene that included frequent showering and the regular use of mouthwash and scented cologne. The burden was becoming too great, however, and Thomas found himself less willing to put in the time and the effort necessary to maintain the illusion.

Upon arriving at Coda, he thought he would take a moment to give Brooke a call. He went so far as to dial her number before quickly disconnecting when it occurred to him that Jerry may have figured out a way to listen in on his conversation, just to see if he mentioned the ghost to his wife. Thomas decided that it was not worth the risk to say anything to anyone.

He worked through lunch and managed to hammer out a sales contract with Coda Pharmaceuticals by day's end. The agreement was better for Coda, with Thomas leaving more commission money on the table than he would have liked, but he was just glad to conclude his business there. He said his goodbyes, but he didn't check out of his hotel. He returned to Rena's that night, hoping to surprise the Alpha Tau Omega house co-president, but Jerry was nowhere to be seen.

Determined to have the last laugh, Thomas went back to the restaurant each of the next three nights, until finally on the third night he saw Jerry walk in with a tall, slender brunette, both formally dressed like they had just left a Broadway play or an opera. Thomas recognized the woman from Coda, where she worked as a laboratory analyst. They were escorted to an intimate table at the back of the bar and sat down. There were no other tables in the section. They were all alone and barely visible in the dim radiance of a flameless candle.

Thomas watched them out of the corner of his eye as he sipped his scotch and water.

And waited.

For the first time all week he was relaxed, at peace. He felt like he was home. In the bar, he didn't have to pretend to be anything that he was not.

When the woman got up to go to the ladies' room, Thomas finished his drink and slipped a hundred-dollar bill under the glass. When she disappeared down the hallway, he slid off the stool and walked deliberately across the room, squinting through the darkness at Jerry, who was sitting there with his head down looking at his phone. As Thomas approached the table, Jerry looked up absently. For a moment, his expression did not change, and then all at once recognition washed over his face. He did a double take. "Tom Boy? What are you doing here?"

"You don't have to pretend anymore," Thomas said calmly. "The ruse is over. And while I should give you credit for originality and authenticity, you'll be disappointed to know that you didn't fool me for one second. I knew all along that the whole thing was staged for my benefit. And I never mentioned anything about the ghost. Not to Brooke. Not to anyone. It seems like I'm the one who fooled *you*. So, who's the clod now, Jerry?"

"I-I don't understand what you're talking about," Jerry insisted.

"Maybe you'll understand this," Thomas said, reaching around and removing the double-barreled shotgun underneath his coat.

Jerry's eyes went wide as the barrels were leveled at him. "No, D...," he started to say just before the muzzle blast momentarily brightened the shadowy corner of the bar and the 12-gauge shotgun shell all but decapitated him.

"The bill's come due," Thomas said softly and raised the shotgun again, this time placing the barrel under his chin and pulling the trigger.

Carl the bartender saw the whole thing. He later provided eyewitness testimony to investigators about the gruesome murder-suicide. He would tell detectives all he knew about Thomas, which wasn't much, from the killer's multiple visits to the restaurant bar that week. Carl said that Thomas' drink of choice was scotch and water and that he was a big Yankee fan.

No motive could be established and the incident was considered a lone gunman shooting by a deeply disturbed individual, adding that there was nothing anybody could have done to prevent the tragedy that unfolded.

The one stumbling block in the case was the question of how Thomas had gotten his hands on the shotgun, particularly the vintage make and model that he had in his possession.

Carl had witnessed something else that he could not explain. After the shooting, while he was sitting at the bar with a drink to calm his nerves, waiting to give his statement to the police, he heard someone call his name. He instantly looked up, expecting to see the detective he had briefly spoken with earlier returning to conduct an official interview. However, the detective was fifty feet away talking to a bar patron, and there was no one else around. Carl shrugged and took a sip of his bourbon, then he heard his name being called a second time. He looked around, and there, in the brilliant white light of a police cruiser's flickering strobe reflecting inside the bar, he saw a ghostly image in the booth where the shootings had taken place. The bodies had already been removed, but the figure sitting at the table looked exactly like the shooter, identified as Thomas Couchon of Boomstack, Idaho, staring back at him and making a beckoning gesture to him with one hand.

Then, just like that, the doppelganger was gone.

A moment later, when Carl stepped onto the sidewalk outside the restaurant to get some fresh air, he realized that none of the emergency vehicles parked in the street had their flashers on. When he provided his official statement to the detective, he made no mention of what he had seen.

Why The Angel Dudley Didn't Want To Return To Earth
Denise Noe

Cary Grant had always played distinguished men.
The Bishop's Wife gave it a celestial spin.
So Dudley hung up the halo, tucked in the wings;
in a suit and tie, he came to guide the earthlings.
Then he begged, "God, send me to the other side of the
    universe.
You know this planet is not the only one living with sin's
    curse
but the eyes and smile of Loretta Young
could make any angel's harp come unstrung."

Inheritance
Dale Kesterson

The voices from the next room increased to where Kacey could no longer ignore them.

"There they go again, Meng-Po," she sighed, stroking her long-haired white cat. "Battling about whether or not to take Dad's promotion and get us out of this hole."

Katherine Charlotte Todd tried to block out the sound of her parents' argument by focusing on her homework assignment. It wasn't working too well, partially because the assignment was duller than her life. The effort failed completely when her mother's voice penetrated the thin wall.

"We've been over this before," her mother insisted.

"Katherine," her step-dad, the only father she knew, argued, "even Kacey wants out of this dead-end town."

"Dave, I told you this was coming when you asked me to marry you. I can't leave Red Cliff, and neither can Kacey." Although her mom's voice was soft, the words carried as if she was in the room. "I can't tell you why until tomorrow. I can't even tell *her* yet, not until eleven tonight. Besides, she's listening."

Her mother was always refusing to move, Kacey reflected as she deliberately tuned out their conversation. She suspected it was why her father—her real father—had taken off and disappeared. Mom was different, and her grandmother was forever saying that *she*—Kacey—was just like her mother. Both of them constantly told her that one day she was going to be grateful, when she was eighteen.

"Well, my eighteenth birthday was tomorrow. I'm not grateful, and I'm not staying," she told Meng-Po firmly. "I refuse to stay here and rot!" *There, I finally said it out loud —even if it was to my cat.*

A knock sounded on the front door. Kacey knew it would be her boyfriend.

"Kacey!" her mom called a moment later. "Jeff's here to see you."

"Coming," she replied. The assignment was going to have to wait—she worked better under pressure anyway. Today marked the day Jeff was going to get his answer about the scholarship application from State U. If he got out, he'd take her with him. She kept reminding herself she was almost eighteen—only a few more hours!

"Hey, Kacey," Jeff greeted her as she descended the porch steps. "Mrs. Clearwood, is it okay if we take a walk?"

"Sure, Jeff. Just don't stay out after dusk."

One glance at him told her that Jeff was excited; she knew the signs. They had been best friends since he came to live with his uncle after his dad was killed in an industrial accident ten years ago. Jeff never talked about his mother. The two had plans—and they had each other. Graduation was coming up soon and they were going to get out of Red Cliff to build a life together.

"You got the scholarship?" she eagerly asked.

"No, something much better."

"Better than a full scholarship to State?"

"Let's take that walk. I'll tell you all about it."

***

Their neighborhood, if she wanted to glorify it by calling it that, was on the edge of their tiny town. The town, which was more like a small village, was pretty close to the middle of nowhere. It was spring, but this year nothing on the high plains was green. The needed rains had not fallen and the seven-year drought continued. Grandma Charlotte had been saying all winter that it was a sign another *happening* was coming, whatever that meant. Her mother always agreed, too Neither one of them ever explained anything like that. As the all-important birthday approached, Grandma Charlotte had been spending more and more time with her mother in what they called grandmother's study. She was not allowed in there until asked.

Kacey and Jeff headed away from town, not their usual direction. Kacey's home was at the end of the paving. The road continued, but beyond their house it was hard-packed earth.

"So, tell me," she asked as their steps kicked up the dry, dusty dirt of the road, "what could be better than the full basketball scholarship of our dreams?"

"I only got the one to the Community College," he reluctantly admitted, "but it's not important now."

"Geez, I'm sorry you didn't get the big one, but it's better than nothing. It will do, Jeff." She hesitated. "I have something to tell you, too, but what's wrong with Community?"

"Don't need it anymore. I have a new job." He smiled down at her skeptical reaction. "Seriously, Kace, I don't need it."

"You have a job?"

"I'm going to be working for a guy I met last week. He's offering all sorts of opportunity and good money. That's why I haven't been to see you these past two days. And I have a house now, too. Of my own."

"A *house*?"

"That's where we are going."

"Jeff, this is the old road. There are no houses out this way."

"There's one. It's not much," he stated, "but it's mine. I hadn't noticed it either, but it's here. Mr. Stoker stays there when he's in town."

"Jeff, why would a businessman stay in the middle of nowhere in a house that doesn't exist?" A feeling of uneasiness crept over her.

As she spoke, he pointed ahead. "There."

There was a house. For some unknown reason, she had never noticed it before. It was a one-story structure which resembled a single-wide mobile home. Not exactly new in appearance, it was well above what some called trailer-park trash. She saw a propane tank and power lines leading into it. She noticed there was no sign of any shrubs or other personal touches. There was a new red compact car parked in the driveway next to it.

"Whose car?"

"Mine. I didn't want to show off in front of your folks, so I walked the way I usually do. Mr. Stoker gave it to me."

"He gave you a *car*?"

"Yup—he said it was part of my salary."

She stopped walking and squarely faced him. "Are you dealing drugs or something stupid?"

"Kacey, I'm not an idiot. I know the people around here. He needs contacts. I can't tell you any more about it, but I promise it's nothing illegal." He glanced down at her, "You have something to tell me?"

Kacey ignored him. She gazed at the house, and the longer she stared at it, the more unsettled she became. "Jeff, I need to go back, I have to finish my homework." She looked up at the handsome boy she had grown to love and trust. "Please, let's go?" She reached up to give him a hug.

He hugged her. "I have to wait for Mr. Stoker. He wants to meet you. I told him nothing was final unless you gave the okay. All decisions have to be made by us both."

As they stood by the side of the road, a cloud of dust came towards them and slowed. It was another new car, a larger one than the parked vehicle, driven by a man she had never seen before. He pulled into the driveway, parking behind Jeff's vehicle, got out, and came towards them.

"You must be Kacey," he greeted her, taking off his sunglasses. "I'm Lucius Stoker."

"Hello." Kacey figured she imagined a fleeting glint of red in the man's deep brown eyes.

"It's no wonder Jeff won't make a final decision without you. You're very pretty, my dear."

Kacey found herself clinging to Jeff. "Thank you," she murmured, suddenly shy.

"Shall we go in?" Stoker was tall, distinguished-looking, and much more formally dressed than she was used to seeing—no one in Red Cliff wore a real suit, not even the bankers.

Feeling her hesitate, Jeff encouraged her. "Please, just for a minute, Kace – then I'll walk you home."

As she passed through the doorway, Kacey shivered, as if she was standing in front of an air conditioner going at full blast. The living room was neat, clean, and decently furnished. She looked at Jeff, suddenly unsure of herself. She was not comfortable and she knew he could feel it.

"What do you think? Pretty nice, huh!" Jeff said. He scuffed his shoe against the rug on the floor, as if suddenly embarrassed.

"Jeff, I really must get going. I have that homework assignment for Mrs. Duval to finish, and Mom wants to talk to me about my birthday party." Kacey's words came out in a rush and she edged closer to the door.

"That's right," Stoker said, smiling, "you'll be eighteen tomorrow. All grown up." His voice was deep and smooth, yet it disturbed her. "Jeff told me. It's a big day. Bigger than you realize."

"I beg your pardon?" she asked, not certain if she correctly heard his words. "Bigger?"

"Well, once you're eighteen you can make all the important decisions of your life for yourself," he replied. "You feel you're old enough, don't you?" His deep brown eyes caught and held hers.

"There are times I'm not sure," she replied, even as she wondered why she felt impelled to answer honestly. She glanced out the window at the darkening sky. "Yikes! I'm supposed to be home already. Jeff? Can you walk me home?"

"I can drive you," Stoker offered. "No need for Jeff to leave."

"No thank you, Mr. Stoker," she quickly responded. "I mean, if my folks see me getting out of a stranger's car, I'll catch it for sure. Nice meeting you." She was halfway out the door when she heard Jeff's voice, but she could not quite understand what he said.

Kacey figured it was her imagination, but she felt as if she tore through an invisible curtain of energy as she crossed the threshold of the house.

***

She ran home—it was closer than she thought it would be—and as she got away from the house the sky lightened. Her thoughts raced. How could that house be there? It had not been there the last time she walked that way, and it takes *time* to build a house, or even move one into place. She climbed the familiar steps to the porch and flopped down on the top one.

"Safe!" she murmured to herself. For the first time since Jeff said he didn't need the scholarship, she felt as if she was. *Safe.*

"Kacey?" Grandma Charlotte was in the doorway. "Is something wrong?"

"Grandma, I wish I knew. Jeff didn't get his scholarship, but he's got a job here in town," she replied. "Did you know there's a house just south of here?"

"A house." Her grandmother frowned and came out onto the porch. As she sat in the swing, she phrased it as a question. "You saw a house on the old road?"

"There's a house on the old road. I've been in it. His new boss gave it to Jeff, along with a new car. I'd never seen it before, but it's there." She shuddered. "I met Jeff's new boss in the house. I—I didn't feel comfortable there, so I came home."

"Sweetheart, stay out here. You'll be safe as long as you're on the porch. I want a word with your mother."

Kacey wondered why her grandmother had used the term 'safe' about the porch, even as she realized she had the same thought when she got back to it.

Less than two minutes passed before her mother and grandmother came back out.

"Kacey, I want to know exactly what happened." Katherine's tone underlined the command.

Kacey related the whole incident to them, from her conversation with Jeff to the meeting with Mr. Stoker, including her feelings of unease.

"Mom, what's going on? I know you like Jeff, even though you keep telling me that he's not the one for me." Kacey hesitated, and admitted, "It feels all wrong. I'm scared, both for me and for him."

"I do like Jeff. I have some answers, but your grandmother and I have some things to do. We'll be in the back."

Kacey frowned. "Can I come with you? I'd feel better if

I could. Please?"

"We're not shutting you out, but we need to do this alone."

"I'm worried about Jeff. Is he going to be okay?"

"Whether or not he's going to be okay will depend on him, the kind of man he is deep inside." Her mother sighed. "This isn't easy for me. Please, be a dear and go inside and stay in your room until I come for you."

Kacey saw her mother and grandmother go to the study, which was a sort of storage building that was always locked. She went to her room to wait, and tried to get back into her homework.

She managed to finish her assignment, which had been easier to concentrate on than she thought it would be, when a storm suddenly blew up.

The sky darkened with swirling clouds. Lightning flashed, but there was no rain. Meng-Po shivered, and crawled up into her lap, mewling because of the noise.

"Kacey!" Jeff rapped on her window. "I need you!"

She opened the sash. "Jeff! What's wrong?" The wind blew the curtains in her face.

"I need you," he repeated, shouting over the storm's noise. "Please?"

"I'll meet you on the porch," she agreed. She fought with the curtains as she closed the window. She tucked Meng-Po into her covers. If Jeff needed her, she could stay on the porch—even her grandmother said it was safe.

Jeff was there, waiting for her.

"Kacey, come with me. Please," he pleaded. "We can be together, go anywhere we want to go. I want you with me. I need you to help me."

"I can't go anywhere now," she replied, startled by the desperation in his voice. "I've promised to stay in the house."

Jeff wrapped her in a tight hug. "Kacey, Kacey, I'm afraid."

"What is it? What are you afraid of?"

"I'm afraid of what I might become if you aren't with me," he confided in a whisper. "I'm not sure I'm a good person."

"Of course you're a good person. I couldn't love you if you were a bad person." She bit her lip.

Katherine came up onto the porch from the back garage. "Hello, Jeff."

"Mrs. Clearwood, I have a new job with great prospects and I want Kacey with me."

"Jeff, I know you love my daughter and you want what's best for her, but I can't let her go with you. Not before her birthday." Katherine regarded the young man in front of her with a piercing stare which Kasey knew well—there was no way to hide anything from it. Then her tone became gentle. "You can stay here on the porch for the night, if it would help you. We've got a sleeping bag you can use and you'll be safe."

"There's that word again," Kacey thought to herself.

"Thank you, but I'd best get home." He turned and went down the steps, hair flying as the high winds played with it in all directions.

"Jeff," Katherine called to him, "it's not too late. Stay. Please?" she urged.

He turned back to face them and Kasey was stunned to see tears in his eyes.

"Thank you, ma'am, but I'm afraid it may be too late."

Kasey saw his shoulders stiffen as he bent into the wind to walk away.

"Mom?" Kacey's anguish was plain in her voice, even with the wind's roar.

"Later, honey."

Kacey watched her mother disappear into the gloom towards the back garage and returned to her room. She gathered her white cat into her arms and curled up on her bed, listening to the storm. Ominously, no rain fell. The wind alternately pulled and pushed at the house as if it could not decide what direction to take, punctuated by flashes of lightning and the sounds of thunder.

Kacey dozed off.

***

The air tingled from a crack of lightning, followed by a

deafening roar of thunder. Abruptly, the lights went out.

Sitting up with a start, Kasey made certain the cat was bundled in her little blanket and lit the candle in the holder she kept on her bedside table. Not certain how long she'd been asleep, she went into the kitchen. Her dad was sitting at the table alone. He looked worried and held out a hurricane lantern.

"Your mom wants you in your grandmother's study."

Kasey nodded. She took the lantern, lit it, and went outside. The wind was so strong she had to bend against it and fight to walk. The small building's door opened as she reached it.

"Hush, child," her grandmother said before she spoke. "Come in."

"*Kacey.*" Jeff's voice, disembodied, sounded on the winds. Her name eerily echoed as it hung in the air.

"Mom! Jeff's calling me?" She shuddered. "But how?"

"Mother! It's happening *now*!" Katherine's voice quavered. "It's too early. It's only ten o'clock."

Kacey had never heard her mother's voice shake like that before, but kept quiet.

"Be strong, Katherine. We can wait."

"What do we do?"

"We have to explain it to her first." Grandma Charlotte's voice was calm.

"Explain what?" Kacey demanded.

"*Kacey!*" Jeff banged on the door, shouting over the wind's noise.

"Jeff!" she called back. She crossed to the door to open it, but her mother blocked her.

"Let your grandmother answer it," her mother advised.

Charlotte seemed to fill the doorway; her slight, straight figure somehow appeared larger than it was. "What do you want?"

"I want Kacey."

"Oh no! Jeff! What's going on?" Kacey moaned. Although it was Jeff's face, she recognized Mr. Stoker's voice.

"Why?"

"You know, Crone." Stoker's voice resonated oddly through the room.

"When?"

"Before midnight," the false voice resounded in response.

"She will come before midnight. Go back now to your master."

Jeff—if it was Jeff—slowly walked away into the dark. Kacey watched as her grandmother slumped against the frame.

"Mother?"

"I'm all right." Charlotte gestured for the three of them to sit at a small round table. They held hands.

"I was hoping for calmer circumstances to explain what's going on. Jeff is a complication we did not anticipate." Her grandmother took a deep breath. "Kacey, your full name is Katherine Charlotte. You are the third of this era's Sentinels, and carry the names of the two before you."

"Sentinels?"

"Or Guardians, if you'd prefer," her mother put in. "It's hereditary, through the female line if possible, as far back as the settling of this area of the country. I know you've wondered why we never left here. The Sentinels were chosen for this task by the indigenous people who lived here." Katherine paused. "This is the reason why we cannot move."

"We three have been placed here near a Portal to ward off an evil Entity which appears to every generation. The Entity resides in a dimension outside our world, and tries to enter through the briefly open doorway. The house manifests around the opening and the battle begins." Charlotte sighed.

"Is it a demon?" Kacey asked in hushed tones.

"Not exactly," her grandmother replied. "The best way to describe the Entity is a purely evil force whose goal is generating chaos and destruction. I first met *It* when I was your age with my mother and grandmother."

"This is your Inheritance. Remember what was told to

you long ago," her mother commanded quietly.

Vague memories of stories stirred in Kasey's mind. Images and voices became clear, as if they had been waiting to surface when the time was right. A trance-like feeling of peaceful calm descended over her, and time lost its meaning as she submerged into the memories.

Finally, she nodded. "I don't remember being told, but I remember the stories. Why does this—this thing want me?"

"Every time the evil manifests itself, it goes after the youngest, newest Sentinel in order to turn her from the Light. *It* sees you as the weakest and most vulnerable. If the Entity can break the chain of guardianship by turning one of us, *It* will fully emerge through the Portal and take charge of our world. Once you are eighteen, you are fully instated. The deadline is midnight," Charlotte explained. "Kacey, you are going to have to stand as one of us, against this force and against what has become of Jeff. It is using him to get to you, and it's going to be difficult."

"Mr. Stoker is using Jeff?"

"The Entity, which has no speakable name, is using both the hapless Mr. Stoker and Jeff to get to you," Katherine quietly stated. "*It* will have them say or do anything to turn you."

"The Entity, speaking through Mr. Stoker, will claim you three times. We must each refute him, one at a time." Charlotte regarded her daughter and granddaughter. "You will both know when your turn comes and what to say." She looked at her old-fashioned pocket watch by candlelight. "We are out of time. Follow your instincts, Kacey, not your head or your heart." She handed the watch to Katherine.

"Mother?" Uncertainty clouded both Katherine's face and voice as she regarded the antique timepiece which had been handed down for generations. "Are you certain?"

"There shall be a price to pay, but it is little enough when balanced against keeping the Portal closed. We shall not let this Evil pass into our world," Charlotte calmly declared. "Together, we three are as One."

***

The three of them walked into the raging storm, which grew worse the closer they got to the house. The wind whipped at them, tearing at their clothes and hair. Kacey saw her grandmother falter, and moved closer to help support her against the building forces.

A loud commanding voice sounded, deep and forbidding, reverberating through the turbulent air.

"*I claim her! The Maid is mine!*" bellowed the Entity. *It* used Mr. Stoker's body, which stood on the threshold of the house. Jeff, shaky and pale, was beside him.

"*No!*" Charlotte shouted into the night. "*She shall* not *be! We stand against you!*"

"*The Maid is mine!*" Stoker howled for the second time.

"*No!*" Katherine yelled, standing hand in hand with her mother and daughter. "*She shall* not *be! We stand against you!*"

"*The Maid is mine!*" Stoker thundered for the third time.

"Kacey! I love you!" Jeff suddenly shouted. *"Don't give in!"*

"I love you, too!" Kacey cried over the increasing storm.

Lightning flashed. Broken branches flew around them. Some struck the women. The smaller ones bounced off. One large branch hit Charlotte in the shoulder—she screamed in pain as she fell under the impact.

"*Human, do not interfere!*" Stoker's eyes glowed red as he turned toward Jeff. His voice resounded over the noise of the storm, carrying inhuman tones. *"What was once yours is no longer. She is not yours anymore. She is mine, as you are."* Stoker shoved Jeff to the floor as easily as he would have a rag doll. The young man lay still where he fell.

"Jeff!" Kacey took a step forward.

"No, daughter. This is where we have to stand," Katherine stated over the storm's noise as she grabbed Kacey's shoulder. "We cannot help him. We three must stand firm."

"This has to start again," Charlotte spoke from the ground. "The ritual must be completed and time is running out." She struggled to rise.

The body of Stoker, totally controlled by the Entity, was surrounded by a fiendish red outline.

"*I claim her! The Maid is* mine!" the Entity bellowed.

"*No! She shall* not *be! We three stand against you as One!*" Charlotte, back on her feet, swayed in the wind with the lantern clutched in her hand. In spite of her bleeding shoulder, the hand with the lantern was steady.

"*I claim her! The Maid is* mine!" the Entity roared.

"*No! She shall* not *be! We three stand against you as One!*" Katherine responded as she stood behind her mother and daughter, one hand on each of them as the wind whipped them more violently.

"*I claim her! The Maid is* mine!" the Entity shrieked.

"*No! I shall* not *be! We three stand against you as One!*" Kacey shouted back.

"*No, she shall* not *be! I stand with them against you!*" Jeff screamed as he pushed himself up off the floor and tried to attack Stoker.

The Entity screeched in unholy rage. With a savage snarl, *It* turned on the wounded young man. They grappled on the threshold. Jeff, already injured, fell to the floor again with a thud audible over the winds.

"Mother! Are you ready?" Katherine cried out as she fought to maintain her hold on her daughter's hand and her mother's shoulder against the increasing tumult.

"I don't know if I have the strength to fight my way to the door," Charlotte answered.

Kacey saw that although her voice remained calm, her grandmother's face—visible in the light of the lantern—appeared drained. Her wounded shoulder bled unchecked.

"If Jeff can manage an opening, I may be able to throw the lantern instead."

"Will that be enough? Will that alone fulfill our duty?"

"I think so, but I want to be sure I have a clean pathway," Charlotte replied as quietly as she could and still be heard. She checked her lantern. "I believe the outcome depends on Jeff now."

The winds strengthened, almost to hurricane force. The three women struggled to move closer to the entryway.

"*Kacey! I'm sorry—remember I will always love you,*" Jeff shouted out from the floor. He rose and with a superhuman effort, he pulled the Entity deeper into the house. The door remained slightly ajar.

"*Mother! Now!*" Katherine yelled as the three of them moved toward the threshold.

Charlotte aimed and tossed the lantern through the small opening. Katherine jumped forward and slammed it shut. She dragged her mother and daughter away from the building as it exploded. All three were knocked to the ground by the shockwave.

Abruptly the winds died as the flames rose, totally engulfing the house.

"The lantern alone was enough?" Katherine whispered gratefully with a heavy sigh. "Mother, you taught me there would have to be a sacrifice. One of us."

"Yes. Any major arcane Work requires a significant, willing sacrifice." Charlotte shook her head sadly and murmured, "I was supposed to be the sacrifice. Jeff took my place."

"Jeff saved me," Kacey whispered.

"He saved us all, Kacey," her grandmother told her. "You, your mother, and most of all, me."

"He was afraid he wasn't a good person," Kacey murmured. Tears fell down her cheeks.

"He was wrong," Katherine quietly intoned. "Deep down, he was the best of us."

The three women sat on a fallen tree, instinctively huddled together, and watched the inferno consume the house. Katherine tore part of her slip and bound her mother's shoulder with Kacey's help.

"Kacey," her grandmother began softly against the crackling of the flames, "normally, the lantern alone would not have been enough, even with Jeff's loving sacrifice. There has to be a deeper tie. You are pregnant with Jeff's child." She smiled. "You must be."

"I think I could be—I missed my period two weeks ago," Kacey admitted. "I haven't done anything to confirm it."

"Did Jeff know?" Katherine asked.

"I don't think so," Kacey murmured. "I was going to tell him today but things got away from me."

"Then line will continue with his blood," Charlotte stated. She glanced at her daughter and granddaughter. "His sacrifice was unreserved, given wholly out of love. He sacrificed himself to save that which he loved. The lantern completed the destruction."

"Love? Is it that simple?" Kacey wondered aloud.

"Not quite." Katherine replied. "The greatest gift anyone can bestow is to give oneself, out of love, to save another. Jeff did this, without any thought of his own safety."

"Will this happen again?" Kacey realized her question needed to be clearer. "I mean, will there be other battles here like this one?"

"Yes," Charlotte firmly responded. "Evil does not die. We can only thwart it each time it appears and attempts to invade our world. We do this without fanfare, without recognition, and alone."

"Mom, I heard you arguing with Dad this afternoon. Will you tell him why we can't move?"

"Probably, but we will talk about that later."

The three women sat quietly, lost in thought. They stayed until the flames died and left only embers.

A gentle rain began to fall as dawn approached. The embers sizzled and went out.

"Our Work is done," Charlotte observed. "Let's go home."

"Nature's Spreadsheet" by Sonali Roy

Dead Ringer
Herika R. Raymer

PART 1

Dallas Charl watched the two cerulean-tinged silhouettes carefully navigate the moonlit rows of the cemetery. They paused periodically to discuss something. He took little heed of the action. The client was new and obviously brought the friend for comfort. In matters like this, the friend always attempted to dissuade the customer of their chosen course. It did not matter. Charl counted on the grief which drove the buyer to contact him in the first place to push the client to make it to the gravesite where he stood.

He waited patiently as the figures approached. The stillness of the night helped carry their hushed argument to him. The seller smirked slightly as he listened.

"... all rubbish, you know this."

The response was choked. "You don't understand. You'll never understand."

"Lana," the whispered response softened even more. "You're right, I don't understand. But I know loss. The pain is terrible, but what you're doing won't help."

"It will!" Lana hissed desperately.

"It's not possible!" her friend insisted. "No one can talk to the dead."

By this point, the pair were a few meters from the border of the cemetery and the legendary playground. Motionless, Charl waited for the two women to walk within arm's reach. He smiled congenially at them, even though he knew the shadows of night would either conceal the greeting or alter it to appear a bit ghoulish. Still, this was the South. Despite the place or time of day, one always showed manners.

"Welcome, Ladies," he bowed slightly before he turned his attention to the taller woman. The smaller woman's nose crinkled at the intense cologne he wore. So long as neither one took note of the other smell, moreover knew what it meant, all would be well. He took note of the small manilla envelope she clutched and held out his hand.

She hesitated, glanced at her companion, and then allowed her eyes to wander. Within moments, they were locked on the item which was set nearby on the ground. It was peculiar, the set placed on a nearby weathered table. She knew what he would do with it. He'd explained the process over the phone earlier. Now, it was up to her. Once she paid, they would enter the playground and begin. Her breathing quickened as her eyes returned to him.

Charl's extended hand never waivered.

As if her friend sensed her resolve return, the smaller woman snapped. "Don't! It's a scam. He'll only steal your money."

The seller said nothing.

The manilla envelope crackled a complaint as the customer's hands gripped it tighter. Desperation hung in the air, her quickened breathing loud in the still night.

His hand was still out.

Lana's friend continued to protest, but the taller woman did not listen. Another moment of hesitation, and then she quickly handed over the payment. She looked at the man with forlorn hope.

Wordlessly, he tucked the envelope into an inside jacket pocket. He knelt down, gingerly picked up the items, and turned to the customer.

"Which was her favorite?"

Lana tried to answer, but nothing emerged. She nervously cleared her throat and tried again. "The slide."

Charl nodded and made his way to the child-sized slide. The women followed, unwilling to speak once they crossed the boundary from the cemetery to the playground. The spooky segue managed to silence any further complaints. The location of the play area right next to a cemetery was an accepted oddity of this city. The macabre history of both aided in their paranormal status. The women clasped hands in order to tacitly reassure one another as they followed the strange man.

Once at the playground's vintage slide, he set the item

carefully on the small platform at the top of the slide. There was a derisive snort when the dual steel toy phone set clinked onto the surface. He set one-half near the slide part and, with reverent care, arranged it so that the receiver was on the platform. As he gingerly placed the second half on one of the steps of the tower, he gestured for Lana to sit close.

The client hesitated but eventually obeyed. Her friend grumbled wordlessly as she joined her, cross-legged, on the ground.

"Call her name three times," Charl invited as he handed over the receiver.

Both women stared at him; one in distress and the other in disgust. The next comment was not unexpected.

"No rituals?" the smaller woman sneered. "No candles or special symbols?"

He ignored her, his eyes never left Lana.

Lana's mouth worked, but her voice refused to work.

Charl was patient. Honestly, he did not know how it worked. He only knew it did, and it drew people to him. Just as he was promised it would. The ability to contact departed loved ones was an invaluable commodity, even if the mode of communication was as strange as a World War II child's toy phone. The service was lucrative, but Dallas Charl was careful. He followed the whispered advice to not advertise, but made sure people only learned about him through word of mouth. It made him harder to track, but it did not take long for Dallas to realize that those who found him were more likely to pay.

Not to mention he was assured no one had an opportunity to steal his 'golden goose'.

"Leah Anne," Lana finally managed in a barely audible whisper. Both women's eyes turned to the item set before her. They waited a few heartbeats before she repeated the name softly. "Leah Anne." After a few more moments, Lana's hands curled into fists as she tried in a normal voice. "Leah Anne."

The trio sat within the abandoned play area. No one moved or spoke. Charl could tell the friend was impatient, ready to speak again. He managed to catch her eye and scowled at her. The night-lit contours helped make his expression more daunting. Her jaw clenched in disapproval but at least she kept silent.

In the silence, the ethereal echo of a bell ring sounded.

Again, both women's eyes cast to the item set before Lana. This time their expression was a combination of disbelief and wonder. The taller one's sharp intake of breath almost muted the second ghostly ring. Her hands shot up to smother a cry before one, trembling, reached for her half of the device.

Lana took it from Charl's outstretched hand and brought it to her ear. Her tears shone in the moonlight as a smile spread on her face. There was a slight pause as the soft whisper of a small voice could barely be heard. Lana's friend peered at him dubiously as the mother's half-sob half-laugh broke the gloom.

"Hello, baby."

If anyone noticed the acrid scent of rotten eggs before it was carried away by the slight breeze, no one said a word.

***

Why did he think he could go on vacation?

Etienne Laurent glared at the well dressed man as he approached the covered patio of the restaurant providing a delightful view of the heart of Huntsville. The buildings boasted the impressive design and architecture of a bygone time. Large carved stone buildings stood as not only an impressively aesthetic wonder but also structures apparently impervious to the eroding effects of time. Amidst the majestic old buildings, new smaller ones began to surface. They attempted to mimic the grandeur of the older residents, but managed only a poor imitation.

Nothing like the original, he thought.

The Locator grimly noticed how the suited man blended well with his surroundings, perhaps too well. This was most likely why Laurent suspected he did not belong. The messenger confirmed Laurent's suspicion when he walked directly to the Locator's outdoor table. The pleasant spring breeze did nothing to alleviate Laurent's unease. His stomach clenched at the sight of the briefcase the other carried, even as a familiar surge of excitement and fear prepared him for what lay ahead.

I really should say no.

"Gutentag, Herr Laurent," the stranger greeted the Locator in a deep voice.

Another accent, another country. Just how many countries does The Collector have contacts in? he mused.

"Our mutual acquaintance has a task for you." The courier set the holdall on the wooden surface. Undoubtedly, it contained the details of the assignment. "She wants to be sure you understand this one *must* be completed. There will be no reprieve like last time."

Laurent swallowed hard. From the errand boy's words, he knew the Collector was still displeased about the conclusion of his last assignment. Though her annoyance was unpleasant, he refused to recant his decision. Whatever remained at Aztalan should stay there. It was not meant to be part of her strange Collection. The bones and the instrument definitely fit the requirements of a desired item to be displayed amongst her treasures, but Laurent's vision while there convinced him it was a mistake to remove them from their resting place. So he dared to defy his boss and told her to leave them alone. It surprised him when she agreed, but he knew that eventually she would demand recompense. However, from the manner in which this job was presented, this would be a simple normal assignment. Not the retribution he dreaded.

The Locator snorted in wry amusement. *As normal as any of my assignments could possibly be.* With a sigh, he extended a hand to grab the carry-on's handles.

At that silent signal, the other man turned and left.

"So much for a weekend away," he groused as he examined the contents.

Inside was a silver storage box. He opened it to find an empty depression within a satin lined interior. Strange shape. It reminded him of an old telephone he saw at his grandmother's house. Body, cradle, and handset. The odd thing was there were two small sections. Furthermore, they were child-sized. His brow furrowed as he closed the box and reached in the briefcase for the manilla envelope and the file inside.

His eyebrows shot up at what he read. The target was an old child's toy phone set. Specifically, two steel phones from the World War II era. The Collector's interest in them stemmed from confirmed reports of the owner's claim the set enabled individuals to talk to the dead.

"'Just reach out and touch someone'," he recited the old commercial jingle absently.

The implications of this information staggered Laurent. The business of after-death communication attracted many charlatans through the centuries. Self-proclaimed mediums, spiritualists, and channellers who preyed upon the grief-stricken members of society. Several different methods were employed in order to convince those poor souls to part with their money or other assorted treasures for the chance to talk with their beloved departed. A rather reprehensible career, the practice endured despite exposure of and detailed demonstrations or explanations of said methods. In addition to people who truly believed in the ability to speak to the dead, there were those who just wanted to believe. Especially after their own loved one died.

The scary aspect of the after-death communication phenomenon was there were true instances of contact. Laurent was not a Hunter, he had no stomach for confronting cryptids and creatures of lore much less going head to head with demons. However, his work as a Locator opened his eyes to the reality of a world which existed parallel to the accepted one. While tracking down some of the fabled items in existence, there were times he was sure he could see shadows where they should not be. Heard voices when he was alone. His occultist contact, Caz, never said much about his time of study and the repercussions of delving into the Unseen. In fact, he avoided it for the most part. Yet for the Collector to be interested, that meant this item was one of the few that actually worked because of a connection to the occult..

If this toy phone really could contact the dead, or seem to, that meant the owner would not part with it quickly or willingly or at all. Laurent's jaw worked as he pondered that. This assignment could get nasty. He scanned the file to see where the target was located.

"Well," he muttered bitterly, "that's convenient. Here in Huntsville." He frowned as he read on. "Near the Dead Children's Playground, no less. Great."

He used the owner's contact information to plan out the next move. Once done, he repacked the items and paid his bill. Time to get to work.

First, he needed to confirm the owner still had the item. Although someone else with the phone was highly unlikely, due to recent events, Laurent wanted to be thorough. Especially if he needed any protection.

"Wonder if I should bring Caz in on this one" he chuckled, even though he knew he should not call his friend. Caz already expressed his deep desire to be left out of any more adventures unless absolutely necessary. He did not want to be on the Collector's radar anymore than he already was.

Still, a child's toy which allowed people to talk to the dead? Caz would kill him if Laurent did not, at least, tell him about it. The Locator plugged in the provided address to his car's navigation, started the drive, and then dialed a familiar number.

"You better not be calling me about joining you on a job," Caz answered without preamble.

"Actually, no."

There was a pause before the ex-occultist spoke again. "So why do I get the impression this is not a social call?"

"Well..."

There was an expletive on the other line.

"Look, I'm not calling you out here. I just thought you'd like to hear about the job."

"Really? Or are you fishing for more information?"

Laurent paused. Caz had him there. Due to his chosen life path, Caz was privy to a lot of information most people ignored. The fact he walked away from it spoke volumes about his strength of character. Caz never gave a true explanation as to why. One time he said it was too expensive money-wise. Another time he said it took up too much of his personal life. Laurent always suspected it was something more fundamental. Given his reluctance to be involved in Laurent's work, and the increasing danger level, it was most likely his friend simply wanted to live.

"Okay, you might have me there," he admitted. "What do you know about the Dead Children's Playground in Huntsville?"

Caz whistled. "Other than it's close to the oldest cemetery in the city?"

"Yeah I know about Maple Hill. What else can you tell me?"

"Then you know about the mass graves as a result of the Spanish Flu?"

"A lot like Elmwood holding the many victims of Memphis' yellow fever epidemic."

There was another pause. "C'mon Laurent," Caz chided. "I know you've heard more. Spill it."

Etienne tapped the phone with his finger as he frowned. "Unconfirmed rumors of a serial killer using the playground to lure children."

"Unconfirmed, eh?"

He sighed. "The only confirmed reports were of child disappearances and their bodies later being found. It did not help that it happened mostly near Maple Hill."

"There are no coincidences." Caz pointed out. "Something to consider. I find it interesting how local citizens wouldn't allow the city to remove the adjacent playground in favor of more gravesites. Then, after the playground was restored, paranormal sightings began."

Etienne Laurent went still. "You always said that such occurrences were not always what people thought."

"Good to know you actually listen to me," Caz said sardonically. "At least sometimes."

Laurent waited.

Caz sighed. "It's more than that, Etienne."

The Locator's jaw clenched. Caz rarely used his first name. This was bad.

"This is all I'll say." His voice was tight. "There are things Unseen, things from beyond the Veil. You know this. Contacting them is never advised, and if you're foolish enough to try, be prepared. What responds is not what you think."

Laruent bit back a sarcastic remark. Caz could be incredibly cryptic. However, the underlying warning was plain. He planned to heed it.

"Listen, if you're dealing with Dead Children's Playground, do me a favor."

"Yeah, what?"

"Find R. Leig, J. Burnes, or R. McKinlee. One of them should be in the area."

"Interesting names."

His friend snorted. "No more than Etienne Laurent."

He frowned. "Are these also friends of yours?"

Caz hesitated. "Not exactly."

He asked the question before he thought about it. "Associates from your days in the occult?"

Another pause, and then a heavy sigh. "You could say that."

Laurent suspected there was more to the story and waited. The silence that followed was so long he almost suspected Caz hung up. He was about to say something when the other finally spoke.

"I got into some trouble. My own fault, got too curious and greedy. Took the three of them to rescue me. After that, I left."

It was less than bare bones, but the gravity with which Caz delivered those few sentences, Etienne knew not to push. He also detected an echo of fear and felt a tickle of unease. Whatever happened left an indelible mark on his friend. "Sounds like you owe them a lot. Who were they?"

"Hunters."

The unease flared into dread. If Caz recommended Hunters for this task, it did not bode well. "Why recommend them?"

"I trust my instincts," his friend answered grimly. "You're going to need at least one of them."

From his tone, Laurent decided it was better to not question Caz further. "You got a number at least?"

"Not a current one, but if they keep to old habits then you'll find them at Yolo Rollo."

"Yolo Rollo? Wait. Isn't that a...?"

Caz chuckled. "Yup. An ice cream shop. Small, in the wall kind of place. That kind of place appeals to them. It helps the guys have a sweet tooth. They don't always indulge, so when they do, they're very picky. Wherever possible, they like supporting local shoppes. As I recall, they spoke very highly of Yolo Rollo."

He decided, wisely, not to comment. "So, do I just go in and announce I'm looking for one of them."

Caz snorted. "Don't be an idiot. Hunters don't advertise. But you'll know when you see one."

"Oh yeah? How?"

The ex-occultist made a rude noise. "You're a Locator. You've been tracking and locating cursed objects for years," Caz pointed out bluntly. "They'll smell it on you. And you, my friend, will undoubtedly detect them."

None of that set well with Laurent.

***

Laurent spent several weeks at Yolo Rollo as he pursued two goals: to find the cursed toy phone and to make contact with one of Caz's Hunters. He used the small shoppe as a relay point because the address provided was a dead end. Since the information to contact the object's owner proved useless, this place ended up being more likely to yield results.

It was not the most ideal place for the first goal, but according to his friend, it was the best place for the second. However, since he did not know the best time to catch a Hunter in a sandwich and dessert shop, he ended up spending each day, every day in the small eatery. It was nice, the atmosphere was mostly cozy, but he grew tired of the sandwiches quickly. There were other eateries nearby that he could sample, and he did so. He was courteous enough to eat these meals outside, but always at the table and chairs closest to Yolo Rollo. At first, the weather was not so bad. But as the winter deepened, the biting cold was present all day rather than simply in the morning or evening, Laurent began to doubt he would ever encounter a Hunter.

As he waited, he pursued the goal of the cursed toy. At present, the only thing he could think to do was to check the obituaries. It was a long shot, but given the item was supposed to contact the dead, the best approach would be to find a sorrowful individual who would do anything to get their dearly departed back. The obituaries yielded plenty of leads and he attended the visitations and funerals. It was a ghoulish practice and he always felt like an invader whenever he did this. It was never pleasant to witness grief, especially when it was honest. Yet, he had a task to finish. He was here not only to observe the grieving but the other attendees as well. He kept a sharp eye for anyone who might be plying a mediumistic trade. The medium themselves would not be here, but someone who swore by their abilities usually was.

The best intentions and all, he thought grimly.

The person may mean well, but in his experience, it always ended in more pain. Besides, the idea of someone earning a living off someone else's loss by promising them continual contact after death always bothered him. The debate of the existence of an after-life aside, it was dishonest for the mere fact that no one knew the truth. He understood why Houdini was devoted to unmasking charlatans, but he neither had the talent nor the patience for that. His skills went in another direction.

Despite the numerous visitations, he was unable to detect anything out of the ordinary. Whomever this individual was who had the toy phone, they were extremely careful. That was not good. It made him more difficult to find.

Laurent rubbed the bridge of his nose as he considered his options. He was fortunate his presence at the visitations did not draw too much attention, but he could not count on that luck for too much longer. His quarry was elusive, and he needed something.

"It's going to be epic!" a young voice announced excitedly.

His eyes cut over to the two Yolo Rollo employees taping a flyer to each window. They announced weekend events at the Maple Hill Cemetery each weekend of October, with a final big event on Halloween. His brows furrowed as he listened.

"Won't this be overshadowed by the Ghost Tours?" the second girl asked as she struggled to fix the flyer to the cold glass..

"Nah," grunted the first as she did the same. "Ghost Tours are in town. This is in the cemetery. It will be G. O. A. T.!"

Her coworker grinned and then caught sight of him. The smile faltered and she slowed her movements, looking more self-conscious. In a loud whisper to her friend, she nodded her head in Laurent's direction. "Hey, isn't that the Stan that's been hanging here for the last month or so?"

The first employee spied him as she looked over her shoulder, recognized him, and shrugged. "Yeah, he's alright." She replied in a hushed tone as she dismissed his presence while she pressed the tape securely down.

The second looked at her oddly, still trying to get the tape to stick.

"He orders his food, pays his bill, and doesn't creep on any of us. Not even the guys. Minds his own, y'know?" Her voice was still a rough hush, but not so low he could not hear. She finished with her task, rubbed her hands together, turned, and peered at the laptop in front of him. "Looks like he's using us more like a computer cafe." She shrugged again and joined her coworker to help with the flyer. "Don't bother me none, so long as he keeps to himself."

"Facts," the second girl allowed as they finished the task. They took a moment to step back and critique the angle of the advertisements. She gave him another look before he caught another whispered jab. "It just gives me chills how he sips the tea everyday."

Her coworker laughed and nudged her roughly. "Ain't no tea to sip or spill, sweets. At least not until Halloween."

The other looked doubtful. "What about Dead Ringer?"

Laurent's ears perked up.

"Aw c'mon, don't tell me you've fallen for that?"

"I'm telling you it's legit," the second one insisted. "Lana told me."

"Lana..." her coworker repeated thoughtfully. "She still in the hospital?"

"Released a few days ago," the second one answered soberly. "Extreme exhaustion, the doc said."

The first looked sympathetic. "Her daughter's death was rough."

"Yeah, which was why she went to Dead Ringer."

"Oh, not him again!"

Her friend pushed her shoulder. "Facts! She said it was fire. Lana actually talked to her dead daughter!"

"Yeah, and I'm a deadite," the first mocked. She assumed a mock zombie pose and moaned. "I'll swallow your soul!" she declared in a creepy voice.

Her coworker squealed with laughter and they bolted inside.

A lead? Had to be. Laurent barely understood what the two girls said, he was not up on the current slang, but the last part was a lead. The challenge was how to get the girl to talk to him. He stood, stretched, and pulled out his wallet. He doubted he had enough cash to entice the girl to tell him anything, but, thankfully, his time in the Huntsville showed him where the automatic tellers were. It would take him a while to get to the nearest one, but this was the first break he had. He needed the girl to talk to him, and offering money for any information she had was the best approach. At least, he hoped so. He had no idea what a 'Stan' was, but he guessed it was not good from the tone of their conversation.

"Well," he muttered as he looked around. "Nothing

ventured, nothing gained."

The walk refreshed his energy and spirits. Laurent guessed he should still make contact with a Hunter, but none appeared despite what Caz said. Maybe none were in the area, like his friend thought. Might be for the best. Laurent was not sure how the Collector would react to his partnering with a Hunter.

Come to think of it, the Locator had no idea what the Collector thought of Hunters.

That thought occupied his mind as he withdrew money from the automatic teller. When he turned to make his way back to Yolo Rollo, he nearly bumped into the man behind him. That startled him. Usually, his proximity awareness was more acute. It had to be, with his line of work. The fact that someone could get so close bothered him.

"Excuse me," he apologized as he peered at the other man.

He looked to be in his late 30's or early 40's and was dressed in a flannel shirt, brown leather jacket, and jeans. Average looking, with the exception of his eyes. Sharp, battle tested, and older than the man himself. Laurent knew those eyes, he also saw them in his own reflection. Was this another Locator? Or...

The man's eyes narrowed and he shifted his weight.

Impulsively, the younger man looked down.

The older man made a motion with his foot, like a semi-circle on the ground.

It was familiar, but Laurent could not recall what it was. His hesitation seemed to be an answer, and the other man grunted. "Pardon me, son," he said gruffly. "Didn't mean to startle you. Trying to get to the ATM there."

"Oh, right." He stepped aside.

The man completed his withdrawal, nodded to the younger man, and walked away.

Suspicious, Laurent trailed him at a decent distance. If the man was who he thought, he would know the Locator was following him. Or, perhaps, they were just going in the same direction. After all, the Locator had to return to

Yolo Rollo in order to get more information on Dead Ringer. If the man was who he thought, according to Caz he should be headed to the same place.

They arrived at the sandwich and dessert shop within minutes of each other.

Laurent watched as the man went inside. As tempted as he was to follow, he instead elected to stay outside. After all, how did one approach a Hunter? Within moments, laughter erupted inside. That piqued his interest, but he dared not enter. A few minutes later, the older man emerged, a full cup in one hand and spoon in the other. He took a good bite of whatever he had ordered and sat down at a nearby patio chair. After a few moments, the girl Laurent needed to talk to also exited the shoppe. She hurried to the man.

"Your change!" she offered.

"Keep it." He waved her away with the spoon.

Her eyes lit up as she clutched the bills. "Thanks!"

He nodded and continued to enjoy his treat.

"Excuse me?" Laurent ventured as the girl turned to re-enter the shoppe. She turned to him. "A word?"

She hesitated, looked towards the safety of the shoppe, and then approached slowly.

"I'm interested in something you said earlier."

She started and then blushed when she realized he referred to her conversation with her friend as they tacked up the flyers on the windows.

"You mentioned 'Dead Ringer'?"

The girl bit her lip, her eyes darting about.

Laurent sighed and pulled money from his pocket. "I'm willing to pay. I just want to know what 'Dead Ringer' is. Please?"

She eyed the bills. Laurent counted two twenties and put them in front of him.

"I-I've just heard about him."

Laurent nodded, a silent encouragement to continue.

"H-he claims to help people talk to the dead."

"And he can?"

She hesitated again. Laurent pulled out another twenty.

"Yeah, he can. My friend swears she heard her dead girl's voice."

Laurent he noted the omission of the deceased girl's name and was aware of the power of names, so he did not push it. "Where was this?"

Her eyes darted around. "Dead Children's Playground, by Maple Hill Cemetery."

"Is there a way I can get in touch with Dead Ringer?"

"I-I don't know."

Laurent smiled and nodded. "I'd greatly appreciate it if you'd ask your friend how they did it. I need to talk to him." He placed two more twenties on the pile and handed them to the girl.

Her eyes widened but she hesitated.

"For the information," he explained and looked at her intensely. "Share it with your friend if you need to. I really need to talk to Dead Ringer."

"That's what you're here for?"

Laurent nodded, following his gut instinct to play along and drew forth a pained expression. "I heard there was a way to talk to the dead here. I've been looking, but he's hard to find."

The girl relaxed and took the money. "I'll try."

"Thanks." He held onto the bills when she pulled. "There's more if you can get me a meeting with him."

Greed lit her eyes and she nodded.

Bait set, the Locator released his hold and watched her scurry back into the shoppe.

"Bad business."

The young man turned his attention to the veteran.

"Dealing with mediums," the older man remarked between bites. "Never a good idea."

Laurent gave the man a sidelong look as he leaned back in his chair. "Not my idea."

The man's sharp eyes cut over to him as he stirred the melting ice cream over the heated brownie. "Do tell."

Another gamble, but once again the Locator chose to go with his gut. "Someone's selling a direct line to speak to the dead. I'm told it's not a medium, but an item. Dunno about you, but that sounds like an even worse idea. Carting around something like that."

The older man nodded as he took another bite. After he chewed for a bit, he managed to say something. "Something like that don't need to be in anyone's hands."

Laurent's fingers tapped on the metal mesh tabletop. "Have to agree." He recalled what Caz told him. "I understand something like that doesn't tap into the realm of the dead. What talks through it isn't loved ones, but something no one should talk to. Much less get the attention of."

"So you do listen." Another sharp look from the other man. "Smart kid. Maybe I *will* help you."

The Locator's fingers stopped tapping. "Caz called you."

"He managed to get a message through," the other consented. "Said a Locator might be in over his head and wanted to know if I'd watch over him."

Laurent bristled a bit at the description, but then again the few cases Caz had been part of had not gone well. He could not blame his friend for being overly cautious. To be honest, after the last item that involved the dead, Laurent was not eager to do this one alone.

His neighbor finished his treat, cleaned up, threw away the trash, and strode over. "Name's Leig."

The Locator rose to stand before the Hunter. "Laurent."

Leig nodded a greeting but did not offer a hand. "So, you sure the little one will provide the information you need?"

"Need, or greed, is a powerful motivational tool. She wants more money, and she knows she'll get it if she gives me what I want."

"You put a lot of faith in that."

Laurent scoffed. "I just know people will do almost anything for money."

Leig smiled without amusement. "True."

***

Laurent navigated the gravestones alone.

Leig said he would be around, but, as usual, he couldn't detect him. If that was a Hunter skill, to hide their presence, it was a scary one. The Yolo Rollo girl came through; a name and a contact number. Before he called it, he made sure to reach out to his Contact. The Collector's errand boy approached his table while they were on the phone. It was truly eerie how they did that. He knew they weren't keeping him under surveillance, because he would be able to detect them, unlike the Hunters. Yet, how they kept popping up like this really bothered him.

"You have a lead, *mein herr*?" the man asked as he put away the phone.

,"Yes, but from what I understand, I need cash." Laurent answered as he mirrored the action.

The Contact said nothing, merely reached into his jacket under the outer coat and pulled out a thick manilla envelope. He set it on the metal mesh tabletop, turned, and left. Laurent waited until he could no longer see the man before he picked it up. Inside was a considerable amount in hundreds.

"Smart," he muttered. "Since five hundreds are no longer legal tender." He had to chuckle at that idiocy. "Well, when everything becomes digital, I wonder how these people will function."

A puzzle for another time.

For now, he managed to convince Dead Ringer to meet him at the Dead Children's Playground. This close to Halloween, it was undoubtedly not a good idea. The Veil was too thin. Still, it was not his call for where or when the meeting to take place. It was Dead Ringer's. He insisted on this time and place. It did not sit well with him, even with a Hunter accompanying him.

"I can't be close," Leig told him while they were en route. "But I'll be nearby. Just keep your wits about you."

Leig did not talk much in the few days they'd collaborated. The Locator talked with the girl, with Dead Ringer, and with his Contact more than he did the Hunter. The veteran merely watched him work. It unsettled him to have someone he could not detect unless the Locator was directly looking at the Hunter as the latter watched Laurent finish his tasks, but he continued until the meeting with Dead Ringer was set. After he was informed of the time and place, he and the Hunter drove to their destination, where Leig promptly disappeared not long after they arrived at Maple Hill Cemetery.

Not sure when the veteran slipped away, all Laurent knew was the two of them entered the cemetery together. As they made their way to the Dead Children's Playground, Laurent turned to make sure Leig was still with him, and found he was not. It startled him for a moment, but then he recalled the Hunter told him he would not stick close but would be around. The Locator had no idea what the Hunter was doing, but he had no time to find out. The assigned meeting time approached and Laurent dare not miss it.

He arrived at the designated area. Ironically, it was the crumbled low wall between the cemetery and the playground. He did not want to think about the similarity. It was a few days before Halloween, when the Veil between realms was thin. Here he was, standing at a measly barrier between a cemetery and a playground, both with questionable reputations. He could not shake the feeling that he was at a distinct disadvantage.

The unpleasant aroma of rotten eggs greeted him before the voice did.

"Welcome, kind sir."

Laurent's attention focused on the figure that emerged from behind a row of trees. He was casually dressed, but moved with a slimy grace that made the Locator's skin crawl. His nose burned with the combined scent of spoiled eggs and the more potent aroma of cologne. In the other's hands, he carried a small wooden carrying case, very similar to the one Collector assigned to Laurent. He guessed the item she wanted was inside.

"I understand you wish to contact someone?" Dead Ringer asked in a too smooth voice.

Laurent did his best to assume a sorrowful manner.

He had seen enough examples in the last weeks to be able to mimic it well. He knew it was essential to have the proper mannerisms in order to keep this man's attention. Dead Ringer preyed on those who lost loved ones and would stop the meeting if he suspected Laurent was not there to buy his services. Worse, if the meeting ended that way, there was no telling when or if Laurent would be able to track him down again. The Locator suspected Dead Ringer changed his contact information and his location on a regular basis. He figured the only reason the other stayed in this area for this long was because of the annual event and the possible business it brought.

""Yeah," he replied breathlessly, and made sure to make his voice shake a bit. "I... I heard you can... do things..." Laurent did not have to fake the doubt-filled hesitance. At this point, anything he heard was pure rumor. He needed to know the item was genuine.

Dead Ringer smiled. "I can offer a chance to connect with a lost one."

He scoffed, but made sure it had a hint of desperation to it. "I don't believe in psychics."

The smile widened to a grin. "Neither do I. Using a middle man is too unreliable." His eyes cut down to the box. "A direct line, however. No deception there."

"Direct?"

With a practiced motion, Dead Ringer repositioned the solid case where it rested on one arm against his chest. With the other he opened the case to reveal a small steel toy phone. It should look rusted and time worn. Instead, it looked brand new.

"A toy?" Laurent asked incredulously.

"More than just a toy, kind sire," the other corrected. "With this, you can contact any loved one who has died."

The Locator stepped forward, making sure his motion looked hesitant. "Anyone?" His voice was softer. "From anywhere?"

The peddler's eyes shimmered greedily in the dark. "Anyone. From anywhere. They don't have to be buried here, though I will admit it helps."

Before him, the toy phone began to emit a soft blue glow. It filled his vision, as if to set a haze over his surroundings. Unbidden, a memory followed the glow. He could smell the enticing aroma of a home cooked meal, heard the playful feminine laughter, even managed to feel the warmth of her skin. The unexpected impact of the buried memory staggered him. Laurent no longer needed to act. The pain was real. He reached out to the item.

"Nat?" he whispered.

Dead Ringer snapped the case shut. The grin became smug.

Laurent blinked and shook his head and looked to the other man. The other's eyes were cold, empty, calculating. This close, he could definitely smell something foul beneath an intense amount of cologne. The rank odor of rotten eggs singed his nose hairs and caused him to gag. The dread increased with the stench. Still, the enticement to talk to Natalie again was strong. The desire to do so was incredible. How many years since he lost her to a cursed item? How long had he waited to tell her he was sorry?

Dead Ringer said something.

Laurent blinked and looked at him, not comprehending for a moment. It was a number.

"My fee, kind sir."

The Locator's jaw worked as he became aware of the weight in his jacket pocket. All he had to do was pay the fee and he could talk to her. Interesting it would be on the Collector's dime, as it were. That was fitting.

The peddler opened the case again, the toy phone nestled within and still emitted the soft blue glow. "Shall we?"

Laurent's eyes never left the device as he pulled out the manilla envelope. He had no idea if it held the amount, but at this point he did not care. One the one hand, he did this to confirm the item was legitimate. On the other hand, he wanted to know if he could actually talk to Nat. A nagging voice reminded him not all was what it seemed. After all, just a few days ago he told the Hunter items like this rarely allowed actual speech with the dead. Something else was usually involved. That fact was unpleasant to consider, and for now he ignored it.

"You came prepared, I like that." Dead Ringer turned and made his way to a grave. He set the case on the ground, pulled the toy out, and laid it out on the grave. He offered the receiver to Laurent. "Just call her name three times."

The Locator looked at the small receiver like it would bite. He was at a precipice and was about to step over a threshold, somehow he knew that. Instinctively, he knew his next action was the most important. If he capitulated to the incredible temptation to accept the offer and call to Natalie, there would be a price. A terrible one. Laurent's instinct screamed at him to move away. Normally, he listened to his gut, but this time he hesitated. He wanted to hear her voice, to tell her he was sorry, to know if she forgave him.

Keep your wits about you.

Leig's words came unbidden, but helped snap him out of a kind of fugue state. Laurent's vision cleared, the moonlit gravesites sharp rather than blurry. He blinked and attempted to back away from the eerily glowing toy. His body shook with the effort, as if he fought against something to break away. The stench of rotten eggs increased as Dead Ringer grew impatient.

"You paid the fee, kind sir." His voice was tight. "Now just call her name, take this receiver, and talk to her. It's that easy."

So easy, he thought, *so why don't I just take it?* His hand began to reach of its own accord. It took great will to clench his fist and push it down.

The man's face turned ugly. "This chance won't come again." His voice was hard now, and held a strange echo. It sounded like another voice paralleled his. "Give in."

Laurent stood motionless for a few heartbeats. His gut screamed at him to run, that something was terribly wrong. He looked at Dead Ringer again, and went cold. Something hovered behind him, or was perched on his shoulders, the Locator could not tell. It was darker than the night, a pitch shadow crouched on the man who stood before him. Its stygian depths pulsed hungrily, and when it turned its attention to him, Laurent almost pissed himself. Those eyes. Old. Terrible. Hungry. He wanted to flee. Unfortunately, he was frozen in place.

"This one can sssee," a hissing voice said.

Dead Ringer's eyes narrowed. "Unfortunate."

Laurent barely registered when the case was closed nor when the man carefully approached. Laurent's attention was fixed on the being. His mouth watered unpleasantly at the overpowering miasma when Dead Ringer got too close. He felt the bile rise and was not sure he would be able to stop himself from vomiting.

"Hungry?" Dead Ringer asked.

"He didn't fall to temptation," came the sibilant reply.

"But he paid," was the retort, "should make for something. A few days, perhaps."

"Perhapssss." The thing's clawed hand stretched toward Laurent. As it did, the body elongated, snake-like. Somehow Laurent knew it intended to wrap itself around him..

He involuntarily vomited while his eyes remained glued to the apparition.

Abruptly, a blinding light flared and the thing screamed. It retracted and Dead Ringer retreated. Laurent heard shouts as he passed out.

***

He awoke in a hotel room. There were sounds above, conversations, and in the hall, running and playing. He scanned the room and took in the bland wallpaper, commercial paintings, and one room set up.

"You're awake," Leig observed and sat down. He checked Laurent's eyes and temp, then placed something cold to his bare skin. Seemingly satisfied, he nodded and stood. "You kept your wits. Well done."

"W-wha...?" His raw throat did not want to obey him.

"Easy boy." The veteran patted his shoulder. "First encounters are always the worst." He chuckled roughly. "Not that it gets any better."

"F-first?"

"Demon, boy," Leig said. "Looks like you got someone who cut a deal."

Laurent went pale and shivered. He recalled the terrible presence. A recollection was nothing compared to the real thing, and for that he was glad. He was clean. Leig was generous with his clothes and bed. He hated to ruin that courtesy by soiling them.

The Hunter chuckled. "Don't be embarrassed. I have yet to meet someone who wasn't affected in some way. At least you got no aftershocks."

Laurent's eyes went wide.

"Oh yeah, that's a possibility, but I told you I'd be close. I had your back. Something I want to know, though."

The Locator pushed himself into an upright position.

"You crazy?"

His brows shot up. That was not the question he expected.

"You ain't no Hunter, I can tell. But you got the eyes of someone who's seen more than they should. And you walk right into a trap without protection. So either you're crazy, got a death wish, or you got a good reason to do something so dumb. Of course, it could be all three."

Laurent chuckled softly. Yeah, Leig was from Caz's world alright. Though, to be honest, he wondered just how much overlap there was now between their world and his. Lately, it seemed far too much.

Leig moved from the bed to a nearby chair, where he crossed an ankle across his knee and waited.

"Not crazy," he managed after he cleared his throat, "just after that phone."

The veteran's eyebrows rose. "The toy?"

"It's a cursed item. My employer wants it."

Leig scratched his chin. "So your *employer's* crazy." After a pause, he went on. "Caz told me you're a Locator. So you do a lot of research on an item before retrieving it. You don't dabble in the occult, but you've already had some bad experiences. Despite that, you're still going around unprotected."

Laurent grimaced and rubbed his neck. "So many different types of protection, I don't have the resources for all that. When not working for this particular employer, I usually select my jobs with more care. Less danger."

"There's always danger when dealing with cursed objects, boy."

He had to admit this was true.

"As for 'too many types of protection', you only need one."

That caught his attention. "Yeah?"

Leig grinned wolfishly. "Oh yeah. And since you got a demon tagging along with this cursed object, you're in my territory. I'll accompany you on this one, and you'll see the protection you need."

"No offense man, but I have no desire to meet that thing again."

"Smart, but you're gonna if you want that toy."

Laurent grimaced. The way the veteran said that made his task sound ludicrous. Maybe it was, but he'd already spent some of the Collector's money to get the item. He had no intention of being in debt to that woman any more than he already was.

One thing was for certain. Since a demon was involved, he and the Collector would be even if he got out of this alive.

END OF PART 1
Join us in September for Part II

ARTICLE

Moralist to Seducer: How Fiction Inverted Dracula
Denise Noe

Dracula lives -- forever undead -- in the common imagination. As Clare Haworth-Maden observes in her book, *The Essential Dracula*, his name instantly brings to mind a vampire in tux and cape, fangs bared, leaning over a prone woman. His intended or actual victim is usually a woman.

Although possessed of supernatural powers and strength, Dracula has significant points of vulnerability. His powers do not survive daylight. Garlic keeps him away. He can be repelled by the sign of the cross. Perhaps most tellingly, as Haworth-Maden also writes, "he may not enter a dwelling unless invited."

Most people know that there was a real Dracula. He was a 15th Century Prince named Vlad Tepes III. He was nicknamed Vlad the Impaler or -- the name he often used for himself -- Dracula. He ruled Wallachia, a country that is part of what is now Romania. He possessed no supernatural powers but, as an absolute monarch, he exercised his earthly powers in extraordinarily cruel ways. He may have been responsible for the deaths of as many as 100,000 people and his favorite means of execution was impalement by which means a person was shoved atop a sharpened pole. The pole slowly tore through flesh until it penetrated a vital organ.

It is also common knowledge today that Transylvania is a real place, a region within Romania.

However, little known or at least remarked upon is the way in which the motivation and meaning of the violence perpetrated by the real Dracula has been curiously inverted in his fictional incarnations. Vlad the Impaler was a stern moralist who terrorized vice out of his country. According to *Dracula, Prince of Many Faces* by Radu R. Florescu and Raymond T. McNally, during Vlad the Impaler's reign, a cup made of gold was "purposely left by Dracula near a certain fountain located near the source of a river. Travelers from many lands came to drink at this fountain, because the water was cool and sweet. Dracula had intentionally put this fountain in a deserted place to test dishonest wayfarers. So great was the fear of impalement, however, that so long as he lived no one dared to steal the cup, and it was left at its place."

Vlad the Impaler's fiercest wrath fell on "immoral" women. Florescu and McNally write that adulteresses, unmarried females who had lost their virginity, and "unchaste" widows were all punished in the following grisly manner: "Dracula would order her sexual organs cut. She was then skinned alive and exposed in her skinless flesh in a public square, her skin hanging separately from a pole or placed on a table in the middle of the marketplace."

Yet Bram Stoker's Dracula represents sexual temptation. When he greets Jonathan Harker, he tells him "Welcome to my house! Enter freely and of your own will!" Stoker's Dracula speaks as the voice of sin, which each person must freely allow into his or her heart. By contrast,

Dracula's subjects, and victims, were born into his realm and automatically under his thumb.

The Count of Stoker's classic novel lives with a harem of three young, pretty women. When they approach Jonathan Harker, he is overcome with fear and sexual longing: "I felt in my heart a wicked, burning desire that they would kiss me with those red lips." The Count discovers the women hovering over Harker and responds with words of transparent homosexual jealously and possessiveness, shouting, "How dare you touch him, any of you? . . . This man belongs to me!"

The Count in Stoker's novel is quite ugly as he is in the classic 1922 *Nosferatu*, one of the first Dracula films (although one in which the name "Dracula" is not used). He is described as an old, cadaverous man with pointed ears, hairy palms, thick eyebrows that meet over his nose. He is said to have bad breath. Haworth-Maden has observed that Stoker's villain has "a physiogomy . . . consistent with the Victorian age's concept of the 'criminal type.'"

Dracula has, with occasional exceptions, gotten even sexier since Stoker's time. While the repulsive *Nosferatu* might have to force his lust on his victims, film Draculas like Bela Lugosi, Christopher Lee, and Frank Langella, are suave, handsome sorts who can easily seduce.

Equally inverted in the fictional Dracula is the real Dracula's relationship to religion. The fictional vampire is instantly stricken into helplessness when confronted by the sign of the cross. Roman Polanski did a witty comic send-up of this in *The Fearless Vampire Killers* when a Jewish vampire laughs at an outstretched crucifix.

Vlad the Impaler was ostensibly a Christian. According to *Dracula Prince of Many Faces*, Wallachia's brutal ruler "was often seen in the company of Romanian Orthodox monks" and "when he imposed the death sentence, he insisted upon proper ceremony for his victims and a Christian burial." He founded many monasteries and churches.

When Dracula showed two monks the usual scene of impaled cadavers in his courtyard, one said, "You are appointed by God to punish the evildoers." The other monk remonstrated and was immediately impaled. Vlad reigned before the enunciation of the Divine Right of Kings but the concept of submission to earthly authority, often advocated by religious authorities, was quite congenial to the tyrant.

Moreover, Dracula believed himself to be -- and was seen by others as -- a Christian patriot, protecting his country and religion from Muslim invaders. The evolution of the name "Dracula" is instructive on this point.

Along with several other distinguished European royal figures, Dracula's father, Vlad II, had been inducted into an organization entitled the Order of the Dragon. Florescu and McNally write that among its stated purposes were "the defense and propagation of Catholicism against . . . heretics, and . . . crusading against the infidel Turks."

As a member of the Order, Florescu and McNally continue, Vlad II took on the constant wearing of a medallion inscribed with mottoes that "symbolized the victory of Christ over the forces of darkness" and a black cape which would later be the trademark of the fictional, cross-fearing Dracula. Florescue and McNally write that Vlad II, and others of the Order of the Dragon, wore it "only on Fridays or during the Commemoration of Christ's Passion."

Vlad II was called "Dracul" because he was a member of the Order of the Dragon; his son, Vlad III became "Dracula" meaning "son of the dragon." Far from being an epithet, the title was a term of pride, bestowed on courageous men who had fought valiantly against the Turks and for the Christian faith.

Why was the meaning of Dracula's violent life been so utterly inverted in fiction? The answer to that lies, at least partially, with the Victorian society in which Bram Stoker lived and wrote. In many ways, the Victorians were a progressive people who believed, as Florescu and McNally wrote, that they could restrain "an untamed nature through the application of science." Although they imprisoned men like Oscar Wilde for consensual homosexual acts, their primary method for ensuring chastity was social opprobrium. As much as they shared the real Dracula's disdain for "immoral" women, the Victorians would have been genuinely appalled by his bloodthirsty methods.

Victorianism was not distinctive for the restrictions it put on sexual activity (many of which are fairly cross-cultural) but, as David J. Skal writes in *Hollywood Gothic*, the separation between "the public face and the private behavior" may have been especially pronounced in this era.

Bram Stoker was a good Victorian. As such, he wished to warn against the consequences of sexual immorality -- and to sexually titillate without ever being explicit. Finally, it suited his purposes to link savage cruelty with the sexual indulgence both he and his society scorned rather than the sexual restraint they championed.

Hollywood has no moral agenda and is free to titillate unabashedly -- thus, the alluring, handsome seducer is generally preferred to Stoker's ugly rapist.

Bibliography

Florescu, Radu R. and McNally, Raymond T. *Dracula, Prince of Many Faces*. Back Bay Books. 1990.

Haworth-Maden, Clare. *The Essential Dracula*. Crescent Books. 1992.

Nosferatu (1922). Internet Movie Database. http://www.imdb.com/title/tt0013442

Skal, David J. *Hollywood Gothic*. Farrar, Straus, and Giroux. 2004.

Stoker, Bram. *Dracula*. Dover Publications. 2000.

ARTICLE

Exploring Occult Detective Fiction with Michael Fitz-James O'Brien
Sonali Roy

A 19th century hybrid, occult detective fiction, incorporates the themes of witchcraft, supernaturalism, mystery, fantasy, and horror fiction. Occult detectives intend to solving cases by introducing characters like ghosts, vampires, demons, monsters etc. that may be heroic or involve villainy though you may not find all these in a single occult detective fiction.

And the entire setting changes when you engineer some supernatural elements and fantasy. So, occult detectives are the wonderful mix-up of the supernatural and the genre of detective fiction. And such literary genre blendings have been very common, e.g. history and fiction, comedy and romance, comedy with horror, and so on. In occult detective fictions, detectives have knowledge in occult. That's why they can solve such cases/and employ such techniques/and characters/and supernatural elements to deal with the cases. But, admittedly, occults must have generated from the trends of spirituality, culture, rituals, mystical practices, knowledge of ancient legends, and curiosity about the paranormal science. From this perspective, societal background is one of the platforms for occult detectivism. Maybe some natural settings like forests, abandoned constructions, deserted places, remote areas etc. may have contributed to the production of occult detectives. It's also obvious that rains, thunders, and darkness have also played vital roles in originating occult detectives. And all these contribute much to the development of plots for occult detective fictions though urban fantasy is also a popular trend in such writings.

A 19th century Irish-US occult detective fiction writer and poet, Michael Fitz-James O'Brien, lived in between 1828 and 1862. He was also a successful attorney. His paternal and maternal grandfathers were Michael. When

O'Brien was 12, he lost his father James, who was also an attorney. At that time, O'Brien received his middle name 'Fitz James' meaning son of James. Later, when his mother Eliza married DeCourcy O'Grady, O'Brien added his middle name as DeCourcy.

O'Brien gained the paid opportunity as a writer in London, but flourished as an artist in America.

A controversial character himself, O'Brien, fluent in French, Italian, and other classical languages, received controversial comments for his writings too. Once he criticized the government and the rich that they didn't help in the Famine. Though not known the exact amount, O'Brien donated some from his fortune during the Famine. O'Brien also advocated for the poor and the oppressed.

Michael Fitz-James O'Brien

O'Brien and R. Kemp Philip, the editor of a periodical named *The Family Friend*, were good friends. And it's for that periodical that O'Brien started his writing career. He anonymously contributed to Charles Dickens' magazine the *Household Words*. He also contributed to *The Lantern, The Home Journal, The New York Times, The American Whig Review, Harper's Magazine, the New York Saturday Press, Vanity Fair, Putnam's Magazine,* and *The Atlantic Monthly*. His most notable works are '*The Diamond Lens*' and '*The Wondersmith*'. H.P. Lovecraft admired '*The Diamond Lens*'. O'Brien's most important surrealistic fiction is '*Horrors Unknown*'. He practiced invisibility in fiction through his '*What Was It? A Mystery*".

O'Brien's short stories are all packed up with an army of possessed Christmas dolls, an invisible monster who was short-lived, glass eyes, robot killers, disembodied organs that carry on functioning with a normal rhythm, quickly revolving ball as found in "*How I Overcame My Gravity*", a telepathist, and a microscopist as seen in his '*The Diamond Lens*'.

> "This miscreant, by means of cold-blooded murder, produces the perfect lens, only to discover his ideal woman in a drop of water. Unable to make contact with her, he is doomed to watch her fade as the water evaporates. He goes mad."

Published in '*The Atlantic Monthly*' in January 1858, '*The Diamond Lens*' portrays obsession as commonly found in Poe's writings. Here, we meet Mr. Linley,

> "an obsessed microscopist who is obsessed with creating the perfect microscope, in the process kills his neighbor in the name of science (because his neighbor possessed a very rare lens which he refused to give to Linley, which was required to build the perfect microscope) and discovers a new universe in a drop of water"

O'Brien wanted to make use of invisibility in his '*What Was It?*', which was published in '*Harper's New Monthly Magazine*' in March 1859. Here, in this science fiction story, O'Brien shows an invisible creature, who stays in a haunted house and targets the victims.

In '*The Wondersmith*' published in '*The Atlantic Monthly*' in October 1859, O'Brien uses robots and speaks of the "revenge plot by old world gypsy Herr Hippe to murder all the Christian children of New York City".

Depicting the themes of obsession, revenge, and the nature of reality, these stories delve deep into urban living. "O'Brien believed that literature could both entertain and educate- but more importantly, with his gothic horror, O'Brien wanted the reader to reflect" (Irish, 2019)

In the story *'From Hand to Mouth'* serialized from March to May in *'The New York Picayune'* in 1858, O'Brien combines the themes of the supernatural and his personal issues with publishing and presents a writer, who is gripped as a prisoner in a hotel, the Hotel de Coup d'Oeil - one with "strange properties".

> "The hotel is surrounded by thousands of disembodied eyes, ears, hands, and mouths, which allow the hotel owner, Count Goloptious, to spy on its guests. When the guest falls in love with another resident who is unable to leave the hotel, the captured writer decides to extend his stay in the hotel, to which he comes to realize that the hotel does not accept cash for payment, but instead, requires individuals to write stories for them – the better the room the more pages are required" (Ibid).

O'Brien has penned a number of stories, where he includes children belonging to single-parent households, as is found in his story *'The Golden Ingot'*, where he speaks of a child Marian Blakelock and her father William Blakelock. William, an alchemist by profession, thinks that he has unearthed the means that can transform ordinary metal into gold. But, actually, he has not made out something like that, but believes so, because

> "Marian is tricking him into believing it by putting a bar of gold into the crucible after he performs his ritual. The reason Marian is doing this is that her father's obsessive quest is killing him. Marian convinces her father that he has accomplished his goal, thus relieving some of the stress on the old man" (Ibid).

Later, a conflict arises between the father and the daughter, as the father suspects Marian to be hoarding the gold pieces. One day, Blakelock conducts an experiment, his lab blasts, and Blakelock gets seriously injured. Marian goes outside to seek for medical help- she wakes a doctor at midnight, narrates the condition, and the doctor goes to the spot for helping her father. Blakelock, after being medically aided with, says that he has formulated some technique, which can convert metal to gold and that his daughter is not cooperating, instead, hoarding the gold. First, the doctor believes in what Blakelock says, although Blakelock's generation of the formula does not sound compelling to him. Finally, Blakelock attempts again to convince him and fails, and the doctor understands that Marian is truly helping her father. In fact, Blakelock hallucinates and lives in the surreal world and becomes unkind to his daughter. Blakelock dies when he realizes that his efforts were all in vain. Here, we get Marian as a strong child character, who lies and sacrifices for the good of her family. The child is portrayed here as the protagonist, who takes a stand to save her father from obsession, although later tries to unveil the truth and gets abused by her own father, whom she loves most- it's truly tragic of her to suffer thus that she lies for her father's health. Besides, Marian knows the truth, which her father does not want to realize, and when he does in the end, he dies. Such stories of O'Brien as including 'Milly Dove', 'Sister Anne', and 'The Golden Ingot', present children serving

> "as the protagonist which challenge the idea of traditional gender stereotypes. But O'Brien does much more than this; he provides positive role models in the form of children" (Ibid).

Besides, there are cannibal spirits possessing a disappearing room, how a child develops a mutual relationship to a grave, and a tree from where people were hanged- such settings really make people scary, which establish

O'Brien had weird taste that he intermingled with different styles- say of the Gothic or bizarre elements in his works.

His other notable works are *'The Pot of Tulips', 'The Bohemian', 'The Dragon Fang', 'The Demon of the Gibbet', 'Jubal the Ringer', 'The Lost Room', 'The Ghosts',* and *'The Child Who Loved a Grave'*.

O'Brien writes in his *'The Child Who Loved a Grave'*,

> "Far away in the deep heart of a lonely country there was an old solitary churchyard. People were no longer buried there, for it had fulfilled its mission long, long ago, and its rank grass now fed a few vagrant goats that clambered over its ruined wall and roamed through the sad wilderness of graves. It was bordered all round with willows and gloomy cypresses; and the rusty iron gate, seldom if ever opened, shrieked when the wind stirred it on its hinges as if some lost soul, condemned to wander in that desolate place forever, was shaking its bars and wailing at the terrible imprisonment.
>
> In this churchyard there was one grave unlike all the rest. The stone which stood at the head bore no name, but instead the curious device, rudely sculptured of a sun uprising out of the sea.
>
> The grave was very small and covered with a thick growth of dock and nettle, and one might tell by its size that it was that of a little child"

The story speaks of a young boy, who

> "never played with the children of the neighbourhood, but loved to wander in the fields and lie by the banks of rivers, watching the leaves fall and the waters ripple, and the lilies sway their white heads on the bosom of the

current." The odd, sensitive boy is abused by his alcoholic parents daily, which terrifies him, and "and his young soul shrank within him when he heard the oaths and the blows echoing through the dreary cottage, so he used to fly out into the fields where everything looked so calm and pure, and talk with the lilies in a low voice as if they were his friends.

In this way he came to haunt the old churchyard, roaming through its half-buried headstones, and spelling out upon them the names of people that had gone from earth years and years ago"

The little, deserted, and nameless grave attracts the boy much. He spends hours lying next to the grave and finds solace- he talks to the dead child as if he were alive. One day, some men come to dig the grave, and the boy confronts and requests them to leave the place, but they say that the child belongs to a wealthy family and deserves a better grave than he is now in. The boy becomes sad and returns home, and at this, his parents make fun of him. He says that he'd be dead in the morning and wishes to be buried in the same grave. The parents find him dead the next day and fulfill his wish.

Such works of O'Brien involve the supernatural elements though speaking of societal injustice too, especially women and children depicted as experiencing challenges and crisis dominate his stories. And I must confess I'd not be able to grasp all the occult detective/and supernatural elements in O'Brien despite my ceaseless efforts in the lifetime though his works demand for other analytical scenarios too in different aspects of life.

Further Readings:
https://www.nature.com/articles/155316c0
https://doi.org/10.3318/dib.006467.v1
https://udpress.udel.edu/book-title/behind-the-curtain-selected-fiction-of-fitz-james-obrien-1853-1860/

https://www.oldstyletales.com/obrien
https://nyirishhistory.us/wp-content/uploads/NYIHR_V20_05-Fitz-James-O-Brien.pdf
Irish, John P., ""Of Nobler Song Than Mine": Social Justice in the Life, Times, and Writings of Fitz-James O'Brien" (2019). Graduate Liberal Studies Theses and Dissertations. 3. https://scholar.smu.edu/simmons_gls_etds/3
https://gutenberg.net.au/ebooks06/0603241h.html#:~:text=by-,Fitz%2DJames%20O'Brien,the%20sad%20wilderness%20of%20graves

–

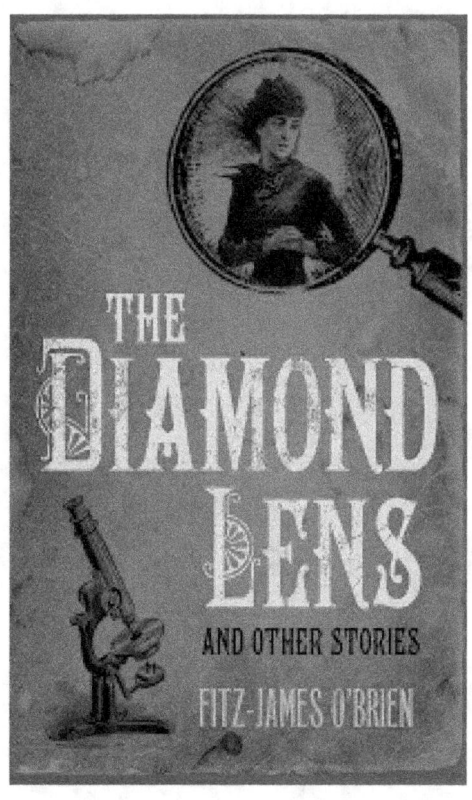

www.ingramcontent.com/pod-product-compliance
Lightning Source LLC
LaVergne TN
LVHW012026060526
838201LV00061B/4474